NIGHT MUSIC

Marian and Georges, world-famous stars of classical music, are very much in love — though neither knows much about the other's past. One freezing night, while sheltering with Georges from a blizzard in an old barn, Marian's deepest secret comes back to haunt her in the most unexpected way, and she soon finds herself in danger from a stalker and a psychopath as she struggles to put together the missing pieces of her life. Will Georges still love her in the end — if they both make it through alive?

*Books by Margaret Mounsdon
in the Linford Romance Library:*

THE MIMOSA SUMMER
THE ITALIAN LAKE
LONG SHADOWS
FOLLOW YOUR HEART
AN ACT OF LOVE
HOLD ME CLOSE
A MATTER OF PRIDE
SONG OF MY HEART
MEMORIES OF LOVE
WRITTEN IN THE STARS
MY SECRET LOVE
A CHANCE ENCOUNTER
SECOND TIME AROUND
THE HEART OF THE MATTER
LOVE TRIUMPHANT

MARGARET MOUNSDON

NIGHT MUSIC

Complete and Unabridged

LINFORD
Leicester

First published in Great Britain in 2013

First Linford Edition
published 2014

A catalogue record for this book is available
from the British Library.

ISBN 978-1-4448-2009-6

Published by
F. A. Thorpe (Publishing)
Anstey, Leicestershire

Set by Words & Graphics Ltd.
Anstey, Leicestershire
Printed and bound in Great Britain by
T. J. International Ltd., Padstow, Cornwall

This book is printed on acid-free paper

1

'It's freezing in here.' Marian shuddered and pulled her coat closer around her body. Her breath misted the air.

'At least we're out of the blizzard.' Georges circled his arms around her waist and nuzzled her neck. His breath tickled her skin. 'Come here. Let me warm you up.'

'That's no way for a high-profile conductor of international acclaim to behave,' she protested as his lips sent shivers of delight pulsing through her body.

'You sound like one of the Sunday supplements,' Georges complained with a sulky look as Marian pushed him away before things became too hot.

'That's where I got it from.'

She loved him so much it hurt, but she wasn't blind to the passionate side of his nature. Like all great artists he needed frequent physical release from the rigours of his schedule, and now was not the time.

Until they had met, Georges was constantly featured in newspapers being ejected from nightclubs in the early hours of the morning or photographed with international beauties on his arm. Not for nothing was Georges Pascal known as the bad boy of music. He had sprung onto the scene less than two years ago and already the more flowery critics were praising him as a genius; but as with all promising talents, he had flaws.

'I can't think of anything else to do to while away the time in a deserted barn while it's snowing outside, can you?' he asked, inspecting their surroundings. 'Love-making improves lung capacity.'

'It may have escaped your notice, Georges,' Marian chided him, 'but I am not one of your operatic divas. I play the piano, remember?'

'That's like saying Shakespeare did a bit of writing, my darling.' He kissed her cold fingers. 'Piano keys come alive under your touch.'

'Right now nothing would come alive under these.' She wriggled her stiff fingers at him.

'Here.' He ripped off his leather gloves and thrust them onto her hands. 'They are too big for your lovely fingers, but they are filled with my love.'

'My knight in shining armour.' Marian smiled at him. 'I love you, Georges,' she whispered.

'So I should think. We are engaged.'

He kissed her on the lips and Marian forgot there was a storm raging and that they had abandoned their car in a snowdrift to seek shelter in a tumble-down barn. Outside, the wind whistled round the wooden building. Inside, the temperature began to rise as Georges' kisses grew more urgent.

'There's a convenient wooden bench over there.' He nodded towards a dark corner. 'We could make ourselves comfortable.'

'What exactly have you in mind?'

Amusement tugged the corner of Marian's generous mouth.

'Taking the weight off our feet of course,' Georges replied with mock surprise, 'what did *you* have in mind?'

'The same,' Marian agreed.

Flecks of snow glistened on Georges' dark hair. It was thick and curly. Much to his annoyance it was also starting to go grey, but to Marian he had never looked more handsome or desirable. Far more beautiful women than she had tried to ensnare him without success, and Marian still couldn't quite believe he had fallen in love with her.

Looking for love had been the last thing on her mind the day they first met when she had walked into the concert hall in Vienna and seen him on the podium taking the orchestra through their paces. It was as though a bolt of lightning had struck her. She'd clung onto the back of one of the velvet seats for support, her legs were trembling so badly.

Of course she had heard about the

4

infamous Georges Pascal. Who hadn't? Not a week went by when his antics weren't featured in the popular press. All the ladies loved him. The older ones longed to mother him and the younger ones yearned to be the one to tame his wild ways.

He continued to ignore Marian and much to her further embarrassment dismissed the orchestra at the end of their practice session, then strode off the podium without so much as a glance in her direction.

Fuming, she had sat down at the piano and, venting her annoyance on the keyboard, she had been unaware Georges had re-entered the auditorium. She crashed to a crescendo then finished the sonata in a quieter frame of mind. There wasn't a piece of music written that didn't calm her troubled feelings. Lost in a trance, she had jumped out of her skin at the sound of clapping from the back stalls.

'Bravo.' Georges ambled towards her, his wicked smile again turning her legs to jelly. 'I think I am in love with you. Are you free to spend the rest of your life with me?'

Their romance hadn't been an easy one. Artistic differences were frequent, and spectacular and long spells apart due to their complicated professional schedules fuelled all sorts of rumours. Georges Pascal had never been renowned for his fidelity when it came to matters of the heart. Nearly every day Marian heard details of another of his conquests, mainly from the women he had spurned who were anxious that Marian should know she wasn't the only female in her fiancé's life.

'You have nothing to worry about,' he assured her when she challenged him over a particularly indiscreet photo that had appeared in one of the gossip magazines. He had been snapped in a restaurant dining with a flamboyant Spanish mezzo-soprano. They were smiling into each other's eyes over a bottle of champagne. 'I have to flirt with my leading ladies. It is expected of me and it brings out the best in their performances, but I would never play fast and loose with your affections.'

In spite of all his past dalliances, Georges was always honest with her, so honest sometimes it hurt. If Marian's performances were poor or she was too tired to give her best, he didn't shirk from telling her.

After another of their robust confrontations, Marian had been flabbergasted when Georges retaliated with, 'How can I trust a woman as beautiful as you to be faithful to me?'

Marian had never thought she was remotely beautiful. She possessed natural blonde hair that she wore in a chignon, her eyes were clear blue, and due to a rigorous beauty routine she could boast an English rose complexion; but the constant travelling and stressful lifestyle would be a drain on anyone's looks. Marian had to ensure she had eight hours' uninterrupted sleep every night if she were going to perform the next evening. As often as she could, she avoided the party circuit unless it were absolutely necessary for her to make an appearance. Most evenings she partook of a post-performance meal in the quiet of her hotel room, watched some television before indulging in a warm bath, then went to bed.

Georges possessed all the artistic passion of his Prussian forebears. Many were the leading ladies and females in the orchestra who had been reduced to tears by his critical dissection of their performance. Yet he had such presence in the pit that Marian suspected they would all have willingly died for him.

'This weather reminds me of my homeland.' Georges eased his long legs out in front of him. 'If I close my eyes I can still see my grandmother stirring a huge pot of rabbit stew suspended over a meagre fire while we all huddle together to keep warm.'

'Did you never think of going to France?' Marian asked, curling her body against his.

'To visit my father? No.' He shook his head. 'His new wife wouldn't have wanted me around as a permanent reminder of her husband's first marriage.'

Georges' father had met his mother when he had been a student travelling through Europe; and after a whirlwind romance they had married, much against both familys' wishes.

'It wasn't so easy to travel in those days,' Georges explained, 'and my mother was worried we would not be allowed back into the country if we left. That would have broken her heart. So one day my father left for France and he never came back.'

'That's sad.' Marian squeezed his arm, thinking of her childhood with her parents and sister in their Suffolk cottage. It had been an idyllic time and it was only as she and Sally began to grow up that the bubble had burst.

'I didn't lack for love.' Georges was philosophical about the breakdown of his parents' marriage. 'I was ambitious and optimistic. I knew one day things would get better, and they did; and then I met the love of my life.'

He stroked her nose with his forefinger. The touch of his skin on hers was enough to start her pulse quivering again, but Marian knew to her cost that for all his cosmopolitan lifestyle Georges could be extremely possessive. He didn't like their long and frequent times apart. Their love for each other was intense, but it wasn't easy.

Marian changed the subject. 'I'm sorry you never got to meet my parents.'

'And now it is too late. How much further away is their cottage?'

'Only a few miles.'

'Let's hope we make it before nightfall. Tell me about this part of the world. I have never been to the east coast before.'

'There's nowhere like it,' Marian leaned back and closed her eyes.

'Everyone says that about their birthplace.'

'Maybe,' Marian agreed, 'but I mean it. The landscape has been the inspiration for all the arts, painting and music. I think that is what inspired me to play the piano. The area is a nature lover's paradise too.'

'You're not one of these twitchers, are you?' Georges raised an eyebrow. 'In gumboots and binoculars?'

'My father was. I only accompanied him when I absolutely had to, and when I couldn't persuade my sister to take my place. She's older than me so I usually lost out, but I didn't mind really. I think the wildlife helped me appreciate the arts.'

'Perhaps we should settle here when we start our family?'

Marian stiffened. Georges frowned.

'What's the matter?'

'Nothing,' she assured him with a light laugh.

'You've gone very pale.'

'Have I?'

'Was it something I said?'

'Whatever gave you that idea?'

11

'You do want a family, don't you?'

'You know I do.'

'Good, then I hope we are soon successful in our endeavours.'

Marian's lips trembled into a smile. There was a part of her life she kept hidden from Georges; a part she had kept hidden from everyone for seventeen years. Marian knew she would have to confess everything to Georges before they got married. Sometimes the intensity of his feelings scared her and she dreaded the possible loss of his love once she revealed her guilty secret; once he could no longer put her on a pedestal of virtue.

'I'm going outside to see if this storm looks like clearing up.' Georges stood up and stamped his feet in an attempt to bring them back to life.

'Do you have to?' Marian asked.

'You know I've never been one for sitting around doing nothing, my angel.'

Left alone with her thoughts, Marian wondered if Sally would be able to make the journey. It was a long drive from Berkshire and it had been snowing all day. They had arranged to meet up at their parents' cottage to start going through their effects, prior to putting the property on the market.

John and Betty had passed away within months of each other. Marian had been distraught to learn from Sally that Betty had died in her sleep while Marian had been on a world tour.

'She quite simply didn't wake up,' Sally informed her. 'I think she died of a broken heart. You know they never spent a night apart if they could help it.'

Marian huddled into her coat. Outside, the wind had died down. If they could complete the last part of the journey before the light went from the day she would be pleased. The weather forecast had indicated snow but the intensity of the blizzard had taken everyone by surprise, and they had passed several abandoned vehicles. Georges, well used to this type of weather, had shrugged off the delay.

'It will pass,' he insisted. 'In my

country it can snow for months on end. This is nothing.'

As she wriggled around in an attempt to keep warm, Marian's foot came into contact with an object on the floor. She looked down. The beak of a plastic duck was poking through a newspaper wrapping. She frowned. It was the sort of toy parents put in the bath for their children.

She bent down and unwrapped it. The head was squashed as if someone had recently trodden on it. She blew off some of the dust. It had originally been yellow with a bright orange beak and large blue eyes, but years of wear and tear had worn away the colours.

It couldn't have been here long, she thought as she noted yesterday's date on the newspaper wrapping. A blurred picture of herself and Georges emerging from a post-performance party underneath the headlines of the local newspaper made her smile. Yesterday's news was today's plastic duck wrapper.

The uneven surface on the bottom of

the duck scratched the leather of Georges' gloves. She took one off and traced the outline with her fingers. Her blood froze in her veins. Three words had been carved into the plastic: 'I Love You'.

Her breath caught in her chest so sharply she cried out in pain. This wasn't any child's toy. She had seen this duck before. This was the duck she had secretly slipped into her son's cot blanket on the dreadful day seventeen years ago when she had been forced to give him up for adoption.

2

The barn door creaked as Georges pushed it open, creating an icy blast of air. Powdery snow fell off his coat as he slammed the door shut behind him.

'I think we should be able to get the car out of the drift. The snow is easing a bit and I've put some grit under the tyres so they shouldn't spin. Are you ready to give it a go? Unless of course you want to stay here all night.'

His smile died as he took in the shocked expression on Marian's face.

'What is it? What's the matter?' he asked in concern.

'C..c..cold,' Marian managed to stutter.

'Then the sooner we get you in the warm the better.' He strode towards her. 'Come on, we can't stay here all night. You're shivering.' He put his arms around her shoulders.

Marian slipped the newspaper cutting and the plastic duck into the pocket of her coat, then succumbed to Georges' embrace, welcoming the heat of his body against hers.

'I'll drive,' he volunteered. 'I've left the engine running. The car is warm. I do not want you going down with 'flu.'

Marian clung onto him to stop her boots slipping on the sheet ice.

'Steady.' Georges guided her towards the car.

She welcomed the sting of snow against her face. It gave her another excuse to shiver. She doubted she would ever feel warm again.

With the traction in winter drive, the tyres gripped the gritted surface. Georges eased the car slowly forward.

'Now where do we go?'

Under Marian's direction they reached Hatpin Cottage.

'What a strange name,' Georges said as they drew up outside.

'A past owner was a milliner.' Marian did her best to sound as normal as possible. 'There's a rumour royalty patronised her creations, amongst other things,' she added.

'Are you feeling better now we've arrived?' Georges asked with his disarming smile.

It wasn't easy to nod convincingly in the face of his scrutiny, but Marian was used to performing under testing conditions and she drew on her professional strengths to assure him she was.

'Let's get inside,' he urged. 'It's a long time since I've felt this cold.' He glanced up at the sky. 'I may have been too optimistic in my forecast, my darling. There's more snow to come I think.'

The cottage was almost as cold as the barn, but there was a plentiful supply of logs in the outhouse and Georges managed to coax the open fire into life. He watched in satisfaction as flames began to lick the newspaper briquettes that were always kept ready in the log basket.

'A coal fire inflames the depths of the soul don't you think?' He sat back on his heels to admire his handiwork.

Marian flicked a light switch. 'The power is off.'

'I expect the weight of the snow has brought the line down,' Georges said.

'I know where there are some candles,' she offered, relieved to have something to do. Her mind was still racing over her discovery in the barn and it was all she could do to act normally.

Georges inserted the candles into the candlesticks Marian's parents kept ready for occasions such as these and lit them. The flames flickered and created ghostly patterns on the walls. Georges' blue eyes glittered in the semi-darkness. He and Marian were seldom alone together, and for the first time since they had begun their relationship Marian wished they had someone else with them now. Georges was far too astute not to realise something was wrong and she didn't know for how long she could keep up the subterfuge that it was only the cold making her shiver.

'Do you have the means of heating up some soup?' he asked. 'I'm really quite hungry and I think the reason you're looking so ashen-faced is because you're hungry too.'

'There's a camping stove in the kitchen.'

'Stay where you are,' Georges insisted. 'Mrs Wren packed up a box of essentials before we left London.'

In any other circumstances Marian might have been jealous of Georges' fearsomely capable personal assistant, but she was a grandmother in her fifties and saw to his every need; and although at first she hadn't exactly welcomed Marian's arrival on the scene, fearing for her job security, she made life a lot easier for both of them by taking care of the day-to-day details of their personal lives.

'I'll have to take one of these with me while I look for a tin opener.' He brandished a candlestick aloft, causing an upsurge of flames. 'Sure you'll be OK? The cottage isn't haunted by the ghost of hatters' past is it?'

'I'll be fine,' Marian assured him, 'and it's the ghost's night off.'

She was still huddled in her coat, and through the lining she could feel the duck wedged in her pocket as it bumped against her leg.

In the kitchen she heard Georges banging cupboard doors and the scrape of another match as he lit the camping stove — reassuringly normal noises against the hushed quiet created by the falling snow.

Marian glanced out of the window. The whole area was in darkness. The only movement was the occasional swish of a branch in the wind. The weather matched her mood. She didn't want it to be a bright sunny day. She wanted to have an excuse to feel so cold.

For years her past had been a constant threat in the background. She hadn't mentioned the circumstances of her son's birth to anyone, but neither had she sought to hide them away. It was simply a period of her life she still found painful to recall. Occasionally an innocent remark or a child's laugh would bring the pain flooding back. In the early days the memory was so raw she was forced to pretend she had a migraine. Eventually she learned to manage the pain until it was never more than a dull ache.

A few months ago a man calling himself her son had written to Marian, but she had been touring at the time and the letter did not reach her until three months after it had been written. Mrs Wren, Georges' personal assistant, had passed it to her with a gesture of apology.

'I'm afraid it followed you around, Miss Barr,' she explained. 'It was incorrectly addressed. I do hope it's not anything important. I would have opened it, only it's marked personal.'

The letter had been poorly written and in such terms as to convince

Marian it was the work of a crank. It wasn't unusual for performers in the public eye to receive such letters and this wasn't the first oddball to have written to her. The writer had mis-spelt her name and her first concern that it might be genuine was soon erased. It was also unsigned. She decided the writer was probably the sort of person who sent out several such letters to prominent personalities in the hope that one of them would respond.

Now she was beginning to regret having destroyed the letter. At the very least she should have shown it to her legal representative, a discreet individual on whom she could rely to keep the details confidential.

She hadn't given the communication another thought until today. The article in the local newspaper had highlighted her proposed visit to her hometown and it wouldn't have been too difficult for someone to discover the address of her parents' cottage. Had her stalker taken shelter in the barn, intending to confront her? If so, where was he now? And how had he got hold of the plastic duck?

'Here we are.' Georges appeared in the doorway carrying a loaded tray. 'Two steaming hot bowls of tomato soup, a hunk of bread and some bananas. A meal fit for a king.'

He kicked the connecting door shut with the heel of his shoe and made his way carefully across the room to where Marian had cleared a space on a coffee table. 'I'm glad that snooty second violinist can't see me now.' He kicked off his shoes and waggled his toe through a hole in his sock. 'She doesn't think I am grand enough to be conductor. Perhaps she is right.'

He smoothed back his over-long hair, the impish smile softening his Slavic features, reminding Marian why she loved him so much. In spite of his temperament he was able to laugh at himself, a trait precious few of their colleagues shared.

'You don't have to be grand to point

a baton at musicians and make a few hand gestures. I've always thought yours an easy job,' Marian teased him. 'While the rest of us are straining to the limits you wave your little wand in the air as if it were a magic stick.'

The soup was beginning to warm her and in the cosy atmosphere of the cottage the threat of anonymous letters faded into the background.

'I am too hungry to argue with you now, but I shall remember that insult,' Georges growled.

'Yes, maestro.'

'And don't go all demure on me; it doesn't suit you. Coffee?' He produced a flask. 'I found this amongst all the goodies Mrs Wren has provided for us.'

Marian accepted a filled plastic cup from Georges. With their appetites satisfied, he adjusted the flare on the storm lantern, before setting it down on the coffee table.

'Are you going to tell me about it now?' he asked in a carefully neutral voice.

Marian jerked upright, spilling coffee down her jumper. 'Look what I've done.' She dabbed at the stain with a tissue.

'Leave that,' Georges ordered.

'If I don't get it out now it'll seep in.'

'I said leave it,' he insisted. The tone of his voice brooked no argument.

'Tell you about what?' Marian asked.

'Whatever it was that was really making you shiver, and please don't insult my intelligence by saying it was the cold. I've seen people shivering from lack of body warmth and it's not the same thing. If I didn't know you better, I'd say you were scared.'

'That's a ridiculous assumption to make,' Marian retaliated. 'You said yourself the weather was the worst you've ever known. I should imagine half the country has ground to a halt. It's certainly delayed Sally too. She was supposed to be here to meet us.'

'I would hate to think you were hiding something from me.' Georges' voice assumed a more gentle tone. 'You know how much I love you, and the thought of any harm coming to you is more than I could bear.'

The intensity of Georges' feelings was something Marian had grown used to. When he was angry, the rafters would reverberate to the sound of his voice, and their disagreements left Marian feeling drained. She dreaded to think how he would react when she confessed the truth.

In the early days of their courtship she hadn't expected the relationship to blossom, and there had been no need to mention her past. By the time their feelings for each other had intensified into love, she had grown to recognise the depth of his emotions and to tread carefully around them.

'I love you, Georges.' She stroked his hand. 'Surely you believe me?'

Despite his Bohemian background, his fingers were long and aristocratic with perfectly manicured nails. 'Sometimes I wonder,' he mused, looking into the fire.

'Wonder what?' Marian's heart began

to beat erratically.

'What I would do if I discovered you had deceived me.'

The tomato soup churned in Marian's stomach. Although her son had been born seventeen years ago, long before she had met Georges, he might not understand that he was not her first love. She took a deep breath, knowing what she was about to tell him could well change the rest of her life.

3

'Now what?' Georges frowned as a tinny overture sliced into the silence that had fallen between them.

Marian looked round, trying to identify where the music was coming from.

'Can't you do something about it, please?' Georges made an unattractive noise. 'It's doing my head in.'

'Sorry,' Marian apologised with an embarrassed smile as she retrieved her vibrating mobile telephone from her bag. 'I changed my ring tone last week.'

'To Rossini?' Georges made a gesture of disbelief.

Marian glanced at the screen. 'It's Sally.'

'Then you'd better take the call in private.'

'There's no need,' Marian insisted.

'You can talk more freely to your

sister without me hovering in the background. I will search out the fuse box. One of us had better make sure this power failure isn't the trip switch cutting out.'

'Marian? Is that you?' Sally's voice was an agitated squawk down the line.

'Where are you?' Marian demanded.

'In a Benedictine priory. It's been converted to a bed and breakfast place and run by an old lady who looks like one of the original inhabitants.' Sally barely paused for breath. 'Talk about spooky. I hope I survive the night without getting my throat cut.'

'Yes, but where are you?' Marian repeated her question.

'To be honest I'm not absolutely sure. Somewhere in deepest Essex. All the signposts were obliterated by snow. When my wipers packed up I realised continuing up to Suffolk wasn't an option. Then I came across this place. Gloomy Gothic isn't in it, but everywhere else is shut up for the night.'

'We were getting worried about you.'

'I rang as soon as I could. I'm not going to make it to Hatpin Cottage tonight, Marian. I've abandoned my car in the market square. I hope the weather clears soon.'

'I'm glad you're safe.'

'You made it to the cottage then?'

'Yes, but Georges and I had to shelter in an old barn to wait for the storm to clear. We ground to a halt in a snowdrift.'

'Sorry to leave you in the lurch. How are you getting on?'

'We haven't started to go through things yet. All we've done is light a fire and get some hot water on the go. The power's off so we can't really see much anyway.'

Sally cleared her throat.

'The thing is,' she began. Marian's instincts went on full alert. This was a scenario they had acted many times before. She sensed she wasn't going to like what she was about to hear.

Her older sister was a restless spirit, always looking for challenges, despite being married and mother to two daughters. It was nothing for Sally to embark on what she called one of her little adventures, without first thinking through the consequences.

'What is it this time?' Marian asked in a weary voice. Right now she wasn't up to dealing with another of her sister's escapades.

'Actually, it's serious,' Sally replied.

Marian jerked upright. 'Say again, the line's cracking up.'

'Was there anyone waiting for you at Hatpin Cottage when you arrived?'

'Should there have been?' Marian demanded.

'Well, it's possible,' was Sally's evasive reply.

'Who?'

'No one you know but I had made arrangements to meet up with someone — a man actually.'

'You're not having an affair?' Marian gasped.

'No,' Sally was quick to respond, 'nothing like that.'

There was an uneasy pause between them. Marian sensed they were on delicate ground. The only time the sisters had seriously fallen out had been over a man. It had been when Marian first introduced Sally to Ian. Sally had taken one look at Marian's date for the evening and decided he was the man for her. It didn't matter to Sally that Ian Rogers was her sister's date.

Eighteen months later she and Ian tied the knot in the local church with Marian as chief bridesmaid. Her heart hadn't been broken. She had vowed never to get involved romantically again. What had hurt was the way Sally had trampled over everyone's feelings without a second thought.

These days the matter of how she and her husband met was never mentioned between the two sisters, but a part of Marian never totally trusted Sally, and that had been one of the reasons why she had delayed introducing Georges to her family. Sally needed constant stimulus. Would she be similarly attracted to Georges as she had been to Ian?

'Why all the cloak and dagger stuff?' Marian fired questions at Sally. 'Who is this person you've arranged to see? Why do you have to meet him here? Couldn't he have come to your house?'

'I don't know how to tell you this.'

'Out with it.' Marian began to lose patience. 'I'm tired. I haven't got all night and my mobile might run out of charge at any minute.'

'I'm being blackmailed.'

The line went dead.

'Sally?' Marian shook her mobile. 'Are you there?' She pressed the recall button but the signal didn't respond.

In a far corner, one of the candles sputtered and flickered. A pungent smell of burnt wax wafted across the room. Hearing her raised voice, Georges poked his head through the serving hatch.

'Anything wrong?' he asked.

'Sally can't make it here tonight.'

'Is that why you were shouting at her?'

'The signal faded while we were talking. She's in a bed and breakfast place in Essex. She said she had an appointment to meet someone here.'

'I shouldn't think any visitors would arrive tonight. The roads will be cut off. We will wait until the morning before we do anything. I've put hot water bottles in the bed, so shall we make it an early night?'

'Georges?' Marian bit her lip. 'Would you mind if I slept alone tonight?'

An angry scowl crossed his face. 'We do not sleep apart.' Realising it would be useless to protest further without arousing his suspicions, Marian trailed up the stairs after him.

Despite the warmth of Georges' body next to hers, her feet did not thaw out. She clutched her rapidly cooling hot water bottle to her chest. It afforded little comfort to her chilled bones.

Who could be blackmailing Sally?

She lived in a comfortable detached

house in Berkshire, overlooking a golf course. The children attended private boarding school. Sally's winters were spent skiing in Verbier, where the family owned a part share in a chalet. In the summer she and Ian could be found in Cap d'Antibes. Friends of theirs had a villa on the peninsula and moored a luxury yacht in the harbour. As a consequence Sally sported a year round tan. She would be an ideal target for a greedy blackmailer who had perhaps discovered something a tad seedy about her.

Was it anything to do with the plastic duck Marian had found on the floor of the barn? Was Sally being made to pay for her sister's past?

Marian closed her eyes, knowing sleep wouldn't come. All she could remember was the harsh reality of having to give up her beloved son for adoption. There had been no one she could turn to for help. An impoverished music student didn't have the money or the facilities to care for a baby. The young mothers at the home were discouraged from hanging onto any keepsakes, nor were they supposed to pass on messages, but some of the nurses were more tolerant than others and let them snip off locks of baby hair.

Marian had managed to smuggle the toy duck into the folds of her baby's blanket. If the nurse had felt the strange lump as she picked him up, she hadn't said anything.

The stark white background of snow lit up the bedroom through the thin curtains. Georges snored gently, fast asleep after their tiring drive.

Marian had thought about turning to Sally for help after Peter was born, knowing she would understand, but she was in Italy.

Marian had tried telling her parents of her love for Valentin, the Eastern European tenor who had defected from his homeland and was struggling to make a living in the West, but they belonged to a generation that did not believe in divorce; and when Marian mentioned that Valentin's first wife was still alive, they threatened to cut off all contact with their younger daughter. Knowing they would never accept him as a son-in-law, she and Valentin married in secret, hoping in time that the birth of their child would unite the family. Valentin had no family of his own and longed to be a part of a loving, caring unit.

After working a late-night shift at the factory to earn extra money, he was anxious to see his newborn son. The police suspected he had fallen asleep at the wheel or, being unaccustomed to driving on the left, he had drifted across the road. Whatever the reason, there had been no other vehicle involved when his car spun off the deserted road and into a gatepost, instantly killing him.

Distraught, Marian contacted her parents to tell them the news, and that was when she learned her father was in hospital. It had been difficult to make out what her mother was saying, but she understood if her father recovered he would need constant nursing. There was no way her mother could provide Marian with help.

Marian's pregnancy had meant she had been unable to work for several months, and all her savings had gone on daily essentials. Without Valentin's support, she had no one to turn to. Six weeks later, Marian kissed her son goodbye. She had been assured his adoptive parents were from a good family and would give him a wonderful life. The duck had been a last-minute impulsive gesture. She hoped his new parents would allow him to keep it. It would seem they had.

Not wishing to distress her now wheelchair-bound father, Marian had never mentioned her marriage or the birth of her son to her parents. In other circumstances she knew they would have come to love her new husband and her son. To tell them what she had done would only re-open old wounds, best left to heal.

Marian had not tried to contact her son. She hoped that perhaps one day maybe he would try to find her, but surely he couldn't be the individual behind the menacing letter she had received? Most adopted children wanted to trace their birth parents to discover their roots, not try to name and shame them.

Marian now began to wish she had plucked up the courage to confess all to Georges before Sally's telephone call had come through. It would be better for him to know sooner rather than later. He had been her only lover after Valentin, but she wasn't sure he would accept the fact that he would be her second husband. He had put Marian on a pedestal of purity. To him she could do no wrong. It was an image that rested uneasily on Marian's shoulders.

Realising sleep was impossible, and careful not to disturb Georges, she slipped out of bed. Creeping down the stairs, she lit the gas stove and heated some water to make a hot drink. Now the coal fire had died down, the floor was icy cold under her feet.

The shrill ringing of the telephone caused her to spill water over the worktop. She had not realised her parents' telephone was still connected. She glanced at the wall clock. It was approaching midnight; not the time for social calls.

'Mrs Betty Barr?' a clipped voice asked down the line.

'I am Marian Barr,' she corrected him. 'Her daughter.'

'Miss Barr, this is the police.'

4

'Did I hear the telephone in the night?' Georges enquired next morning over breakfast.

Marian poured a second cup of tea. The power hadn't yet been restored and they had again been obliged to use the camping stove to heat up some water. 'It was actually a call for my mother,' she said, dunking a tea bag into her mug.

'You poor thing. I suppose there must still be people who do not know of her death.'

Georges slid a hand across the table. His skin was warm against hers, his blue eyes full of gentle concern. Marian returned the pressure of his fingers. 'I shall have to go through her address book but I'm not sure where it is.'

Georges now traced his fingers along Marian's. 'You need to warm up first, my darling. When are they going to put the power back on?' he asked with an irritated sigh.

As he spoke, the fridge hummed into life.

'Someone at the national grid is listening to me,' he said, his sigh turning into a light laugh. 'What say I make sure the pump in the boiler is working so we at least have some warm water in case the power goes down again?'

'I'll help.'

'No. I insist you sit there. There are dark circles under your eyes. You don't look as though you got a wink of sleep last night. It won't take me long. Then we'll tackle the attic together.'

Alone in the kitchen, Marian sipped her tea. She didn't like keeping things from Georges, but she couldn't tell him the call had been from the police before she first spoke to Sally to find out what was going on. Taking advantage of his temporary absence, she swiftly dialled her sister's mobile number.

'I survived the night,' Sally answered on the second ring, 'without meeting any ghosts. There are several other marooned travellers here and I've had breakfast with a sales rep. He sells stationery supplies and he's given me a set of promotional pencils with 'Sally' embossed in gold letters on them.'

'Sally,' Marian stemmed the flow of her inane chatter, 'I had the police on the telephone last night.'

'What was that?' Sally asked. 'Did you say the police?'

'An abandoned jacket was found down on the beach.'

'Our bit of beach?' Sally asked after such a long pause Marian thought the line had gone down.

'Yes.'

Hatpin Cottage was a short cycle ride from a small cove, and when they were young Sally and Marian used to go down there in fine weather to swim or laze on the sand. Later, Sally used to insist on going down on her own. Marian suspected she went there to meet boyfriends. It was after that when their lives began to go in different directions.

'Why were the police calling you?'

'The telephone number of Hatpin Cottage was on a scrap of paper in the pocket of the jacket.'

'It's nothing to do with me.' Sally was quick to deny any connection.

'Do you know what it's all about?' Marian demanded, not believing her sister's denial.

'It can't be my visitor.' Sally was speaking fast now as if she didn't want to be interrupted. 'Why did you think it was?'

'I didn't say I did.'

'Did he turn up, by the way?'

'Who?'

'The man I was due to meet.'

'No he didn't. Sally,' Marian raised her voice as her sister sounded as though she were about to launch into another incomprehensible explanation, 'what is going on?'

'Nothing.'

Marian detected a mulish note of stubbornness in her sister's voice. 'You told me last night you were being blackmailed.'

'I never said any such thing. You must have misheard me. Look, I don't want to waste your battery charge. We'll talk later.'

Before Marian had a chance to say the power was back on, Sally cut the call. She dialled back immediately but only got a recorded voice mail message inviting her to leave her name and number.

'All done.' Georges came back into the kitchen. 'Not another call?' He looked down at the table to where Marian had put her mobile.

'I was checking up on Sally,' she explained.

'As long as that's all it was.' Georges frowned.

'Who else would I be calling?' Marian snapped. She was in no mood to deal with Georges' jealousy today.

'You tell me. Something's going on.

46

I'm not a fool. Remember, I grew up in a regime of secrecy and half-truths, and I know when someone is hiding something. You, my darling, are guilty of that offence. So what gives?'

'It was the police on the telephone last night,' Marian admitted.

'What did they want?'

'They found a jacket on the beach with my parents' telephone number in one of the pockets.'

'And you telephoned Sally to see if the jacket belonged to her mystery visitor?'

Marian realised she had been foolish to think she could pull the wool over Georges' eyes. Given his background, he could detect every nuance of a cover-up and subterfuge.

'She said it didn't.'

'Then who is this man she was supposed to meet?'

'She cut me off before I could find out and now she's diverting all calls.'

'When I finally meet this sister of yours I intend giving her a piece of my mind,' Georges said with an angry frown. 'I won't have you worried like this.'

'Sally's always been high-maintenance.' Marian attempted to explain her sister's actions.

'It seems to me she doesn't have enough to do. You, my darling, are a busy professional woman. We haven't got time for silly secrets.'

Marian swallowed down a nervous lump in her throat as she thought of her own secret.

'What are the police going to do now?' Georges asked.

'For the moment, nothing. The officer said, until something else happens.'

'Like a body being washed up on the beach?' Georges interrupted her.

'Or someone claims the coat.'

'Last night was hardly the time to go walking on the beach without a coat,' Georges said, 'or for a late-night swim.'

Marian glanced out of the window. 'It's snowing again.'

'At least we're a bit warmer.' Georges put a hand on a radiator. 'I can feel heat coming through already.'

'What do we do about Sally?'

'I suggest we leave her to contact us. If you've finished your breakfast we may as well make a start on what we came down here to do.'

The attic was surprisingly tidy. Apart from the usual jumble of discarded suitcases, old carpets and a broken television set, the only item of any interest was a large trunk.

Georges coughed as a shower of dust cascaded off the lid when he lifted it up. 'This thing hasn't been opened for years,' he said, wiping his eyes.

They both peered inside. 'Old clothes?' He held up a battered straw hat that had once boasted an array of sunflowers around the brim. Marian shook out an old army great coat. The buttons were tarnished and there was evidence of moth activity.

'How on earth can we dispose of this?' she asked.

'I don't know. With a bit of laundering, a theatrical agent might be interested. It's period stuff.' Georges was now sporting a scarlet feather boa and dangling some beads through his fingers. 'Carmen?' he queried, going into a rough rendition of the entrance of the toreadors.

'Spare my ears,' Marian pleaded.

'I am better waving my stick at the orchestra,' Georges acknowledged, 'and leaving them to make the music.' He looked around the mess. 'Is there anything of sentiment that you would like to keep?'

'I don't think so, but I can't throw anything out until Sally's had a chance to look at it. I had hoped she would be here to help.'

Georges stood up and peered through the skylight. 'I have to be in Salzburg by the end of the week. I hope the weather will have cleared by then. What are your immediate plans?'

'I've put the next few days aside to deal with family matters. Then there are the details of the charity concert to be discussed with the committee.'

Georges was heavily involved in a charity for disadvantaged third world children and helped out as often as his commitments would allow. The latest proposal was a gala concert at which he and Marian would be the main attractions. Most of the behind-the-scenes work was done by the organisers and an army of volunteers, but negotiations had now reached the stage of needing serious input from Marian and Georges. It was for this reason that her local newspaper had interviewed Marian, and why she and Georges had featured prominently on the front of *The Gazette*.

The programme needed to be finalised, and a tentative meeting had been arranged between them and the charity for the coming week. The country house chosen for the venue was not far from Hatpin Cottage, and it had seemed a good idea to combine the visit to Marian's parents' cottage with an update meeting at Saltway Manor.

'See what you can arrange with the agents,' Georges said. 'Meanwhile, I don't know about you, but I am growing hungry and we don't have much food in the house. Shall I battle out to see what I can find?'

'Is it safe to drive?' Marian asked.

'I'll be careful.'

'There's a mini supermarket about three miles away.'

'Then I'll go in search of essentials.' Georges threw her one of his dazzling smiles. Marian had seen it charm even the crustiest of organisers out of their bad mood when things were falling down around them. He always managed to get the best out of people no matter the circumstances, and that was another reason why Marian loved him so much.

They clambered down the attic steps and Georges shrugged himself into the army great coat. 'I told you it would come in useful.'

'What do you think you look like?'

Marian laughed as he fastened the buttons.

'It may be old, but it's warm, and it'll serve my purpose. Besides, everyone will have far too much on their minds today to spare me a second look.' He delved into the pocket. 'Love letters?' He pulled out a bundle of envelopes. 'Here you are. You can go through them. It'll give you something to pass the time. Don't come outside,' he said, wrapping a scarf round his neck. 'We don't want you catching cold.'

Marian watched him drive off from behind the front room window. After he'd gone, the cottage was eerily silent.

Making another mug of tea, Marian perched on the sofa and opened the first letter. She didn't like to pry into private correspondence, but neither did she want to throw out anything important. A sad smile curved her lips as she read the love letter her father had written to her mother before they were married. There were several in the same vein. She put them carefully to one side.

The sound of a ringtone disturbed the silence. It wasn't the Rossini overture that Georges had complained about last night. She delved under a cushion and came across Georges' mobile. She grimaced. The caller display indicated Richard Walton on the line. He was not one of her favourite people, but he was Georges' agent. She would have to answer it.

'Marian?' he barked at her. 'Where are you?'

'In deepest Suffolk.' She hadn't really been expecting a greeting from Richard, but it would have been nice if he'd bothered to say good morning.

'Where's Georges?'

'Gone to get some provisions. Can I help?'

'His Salzburg date has been brought forward. They need him immediately. This is most inconvenient.' He sounded annoyed, almost as if he blamed Marian for the bad weather.

'I'm sorry, Richard; snow does disrupt things. As soon as Georges gets back I'll pass on your message.'

'Give me your grid reference.'

'I don't have it,' Marian admitted.

'Post code?'

Marian complied with his second request.

'I'll see if I can arrange an air transfer. Is there anywhere a helicopter could land?'

'There's the field opposite. Can helicopters land in bad weather?' She got up and looked out of the window.

Richard ignored her question. 'I'll ring again when I've arranged an air lift.'

Marian blinked as Richard cut the connection. Shaking her head, she tossed Georges' mobile back onto the sofa, settled down again and opened another envelope. The letter was from Sally to their mother. It was dated two days before Marian's son had been born, when Sally was supposed to have been in Italy. It had an English postmark.

Intrigued, Marian read on. Her curiosity turned to shock as she learned that Sally had been granted an early release date for good behaviour and that she expected to be home within the next few days.

All the warmth left Marian's body.

Sally hadn't been in Italy at all. She had been in prison.

5

Brian shivered in the cold as he watched Georges Pascal drive away from Hatpin Cottage. Snow slid off an overhanging branch and landed on his coat collar, then trickled inside the neck of his shirt. His eyes narrowed. Once he had his hands on Marian's money there would be no more sleeping in the back of cold vans and standing around in the snow.

He would be rich beyond his wildest dreams. And when he was, all those who had stood in his way would pay the price. An ugly smile crossed his face at the prospect of revenge.

A shaft of pale sunlight was beginning to melt some of the snow, but the thaw was too late for his purposes. He was way behind with his deliveries and it looked as though Marian's schedule had been disrupted, too. According to that newspaper interview, she was supposed to be at Saltway Manor this week, but he doubted she would make it.

Brian narrowed his close-set brown eyes to get a better view of Marian seated in the living room of her parents' cottage, her head bent forward as if she were reading something. She was nice and snug in the warm while he was out in the cold. Being out in the cold was the story of his life. He shook wet snow off his floppy fringe. All that was about to change, if everything went according to plan — and he had planned exactly what he was going to do, down to the smallest detail.

For weeks he had ensured his deliveries took him in the area of Hatpin Cottage. It hadn't been easy but he had managed it. It was important not to leave room for error. He'd gone through too much to back out now. Marian must be made to pay for what she had done.

He craned his neck. She had

disappeared from view. He ducked down as she appeared at the window. She was talking to someone on the telephone. Brian could hear water dripping as the temperature continued to rise. Already the snow was turning mushy underfoot.

Was Marian thinking of driving back to her smart Docklands pied-à-terre? Would Georges go with her? Brian knew he was scheduled to be in Salzburg during the coming week. He had the details of both their timetables at his fingertips.

Brian ducked down again as he heard a car approaching. Georges was returning with the groceries. Brian pushed back the cuff of his anorak to check his wristwatch. He could spare a few more minutes, then after that he was out of here.

'I'm back,' Georges called through from the hall, shedding the army greatcoat. 'Pah. This thing smells dreadful. I could only get a bit of milk and a stale loaf of bread. I grabbed a bag of potatoes and some onions. I know it's not much,' he laughed, 'but my mother had to survive on less. Darling? Where are you?'

'Richard's been on the telephone.' Again struggling to maintain her composure, Marian greeted him with the news, 'You're wanted in Salzburg.'

'My booking isn't until next week.'

'Things have been re-scheduled. Richard is arranging an air transfer for you.'

'This is ridiculous.' Georges made a sweeping gesture of annoyance with his arms, narrowly missing toppling a vase. 'Aren't I to be allowed any time off? Genius has to be refuelled.'

'I did try to tell him but you know Richard.' Georges was nothing if not modest, Marian thought, and she wished they didn't have to go through this charade every time his workload was rescheduled.

'You can call him back and tell him I'm not going.' Georges now crossed his arms and planted his feet firmly on the floor, an immovable expression on his face.

'Yes you are,' Marian insisted, hoping they weren't in for a scene.

It was a situation they had been through many times before. Plans were often changed or cancelled at short notice; it was the nature of the profession. Marian knew Georges hated to let anyone down. Despite his bad boy reputation, he was the consummate professional. That was why he was one of the most respected conductors of his generation. It wasn't only his talent that opened doors: in a world of temperament, he was only temperamental when the occasion arose. Marian knew he wanted to go to Salzburg, but out of loyalty he felt he had to make a stand and stay with her in Hatpin Cottage. He needed her to persuade him otherwise, and right now after the shock she had just had she wasn't sure she was up to the task.

'I've plenty to do here to keep me busy,' she insisted.

Although she dreaded being alone in the cottage at the mercy of a potential stalker, it would place too great a strain on her powers of invention to have Georges stay; and until she had spoken to Sally, she couldn't tell him anything about all that was going on in her personal life.

'What about the charity gala?' Georges demanded. 'And the meeting with the committee?'

'I can talk to the organisers just as well as you,' Marian insisted. 'They'll understand.'

'I can't leave you to sort through your mother's things on your own,' Georges pressed, the truculent expression still on his face.

'It's not your problem. You have other priorities.'

In the distance they heard the faint whine of a helicopter growing louder.

'You'd better get your stuff together.' Marian pushed Georges towards the stairs. 'You know Richard doesn't like to be kept waiting, and I doubt the pilot will want to linger in these conditions.'

'You're not trying to get rid of me, are you?' Georges still didn't look entirely convinced.

'I didn't invent the call from Richard and I certainly didn't arrange a helicopter air lift.'

'You know what I mean,' Georges said, his eyes narrowing to suspicious slits.

'I haven't a clue what you're on about. Now are you going to Salzburg or not?'

'Not until you tell me what's going on.'

Marian closed her eyes. She didn't know where to start, but now was not the time to open up to Georges.

'I'll see you in Paris,' she promised by way of compromise.

'Paris?' he queried with a confused frown.

'Don't you remember? We arranged a break together after Salzburg?'

'I don't even know where I'm supposed to be tomorrow.' Georges had to raise his voice against the noise of the helicopter as it began losing height.

'Get a move on,' Marian urged him.

By now the helicopter was hovering. Marian ran to the door and signalled to the pilot that Georges would be with him in a few moments. He waved his acknowledgement. Marian stepped back into the warmth of the hall. The whirring blades created a mini shower as they disturbed the top of a hedge, sending clods of snow into the air.

Finally giving in to her persuasion, Georges disappeared upstairs. Moments later he raced back down, clutching a badly packed overnight bag.

'My coat, where did I put it?' He began searching frantically in the hall cupboard.

'Here.' Marian found it and thrust his arms into the sleeves. Georges used the opportunity to embrace her. Like everything else about him, Georges' kisses were passionate. The touch of his lips warmed hers and set Marian's fingertips on fire. He smelt of snow and musty greatcoat. Flattened against the wall, there was no way Marian could ease the pressure of his body against hers. Due to the power cut he hadn't shaved that morning, and his stubble was rough against her cheek. The sensation inflamed her senses.

'Georges.' Her protest came out as a moan.

'What?' His response was a raspy growl.

'Not now,' she insisted through gritted teeth.

'I can't think of a better time, can you?' His eyes glittered dangerously, signifying his need of her.

Marian could, but she didn't want to. Like others of his profession, Georges was extremely physical. The artist in him needed frequent release for his passions and sometimes Marian feared if she didn't give in to him every time he wanted to make love to her he would look elsewhere.

After her marriage to Valentin she hadn't thought she could ever love another man, and she was still getting over the shock of discovering Georges could arouse similar passions in her; but until she told Georges about Valentin, she felt as though she was skating on thin ice.

'See you in Paris,' she said firmly.

'The city of lovers,' he said slowly, his meaning more than clear.

The ringtone of his mobile interrupted them. Reluctantly, he released his hold of her.

'You left it on the sofa.' Marian nudged him as he searched helplessly in his coat pockets. 'I expect Richard is wondering where you are. I'll get it for you. Then you must go.'

'Hello?' Georges barked at his agent after Marian thrust the phone into his hand. 'On my way,' he replied. 'Yes, it's here. It landed a few moments ago.' He was now striding out of the cottage.

Marian was used to his mercurial changes of focus, but today even she was surprised how suddenly and completely he had dismissed thoughts of Paris and his love for her from his mind. As he clambered into the passenger seat of the helicopter, Marian also suspected he had forgotten about her. He didn't look up or wave goodbye as the helicopter gained height, circled and flew off into the distance. Marian stayed where she was until it was no more than a dot in the sky.

A shadowy movement behind the hedge caught the corner of her eye. 'Hello? Is anyone there?' she called out.

A blackbird landed on the hedge, shaking snow off its branches, and began to sing. Doing her best convince herself it must have been melting snow that had spooked her, Marian retreated indoors, bolting the lock firmly behind her.

'Sally?' she picked up the cottage telephone on its second ring.

'No it isn't Sally,' the menacing male voice replied.

'Who is this?' Marian demanded.

'Does the name Peter mean anything to you?'

'Peter, is that you?' Marian asked with a hysterical sob.

For years she had dreamed of this moment, but never had she imagined her son would sound as hard as the voice talking to her down the line.

Outside she heard a car pull up.

'Looks like you've got a visitor. I'm going to have to cut short our call but I'll be in touch again soon — very soon.'

6

Marian raced to the door and opened it. Sally jumped out of her car almost before the engine had stopped running. She looked as elegant as always despite the weather conditions. Her urchin-cut hair was freshly styled and highlighted with blonde streaks and her tan had recently been topped up, Marian presumed on one of her skiing trips to Verbier.

'Made it, at last. Got my wipers fixed and here I am.' Sally waved and ran towards her, checking her step as she took in the expression on her sister's face. 'Whatever's wrong? You're as white as a sheet.'

Marian was enveloped in a scented hug. The fake fur collar of Sally's coat tickled Marian's nose, making her sneeze.

'Come on.' Sally immediately took

charge of the situation. 'Let's get you inside. Was that helicopter I saw circling above the cottage anything to do with your famous fiancé, Georges Pascal?'

'He was called away to Salzburg at short notice.'

'Good.' Sally gave a brisk nod. 'We don't want any eavesdroppers.'

Her eyes fell on the abandoned shopping. 'I see you managed to get milk.' She revealed expensively whitened teeth as she smiled at her younger sister. 'Think I'll pass on the potatoes.' She patted her taut stomach. 'Too much fattening apple strudel and cream last week. Let's get some coffee on the go. I am dying for a cup.' She peered into the living room and took in the scattered correspondence on the carpet. 'Sorry I wasn't here to help you earlier. For goodness sake, sit down before you fall down. You look as though your legs are about to give out on you. I won't be a moment. We've got heaps to get through.'

Marian sank into the softness of the

sofa and held her head in her hands while Sally bustled off towards the kitchen. Through the open door she heard her filling the jug kettle with water and unscrewing the lid on the coffee jar.

They were being stalked. There was no other word for it. How else could the caller have known of Sally's arrival at the cottage? Was he still out there spying on them?

'Sally?' she called out urgently as things went quiet in the kitchen.

'Still here,' she called back. Marian heard the clunk of the fridge door handle. 'I'm putting the milk away. *Voilà*.' Sally entered the room carrying a tray of coffee. 'I am more than ready for this, I can tell you. What a journey I've had. I didn't dare stop in case I couldn't get the car going again. Actually once I started out it wasn't too bad, but late yesterday afternoon was the pits. I could not see through the windscreen. That's when I decided to throw in the towel. Glad the power is

71

back on.' She looked appreciatively around the room. 'Lines are down all over the country.'

'Sally.' Marian tugged her arm.

'Steady, you'll spill the coffee.'

'Did you see anyone lurking about outside?'

'Is that what's robbed your face of colour?' Sally raised her eyebrows over the rim of her mug, a wary expression in her eyes.

'I've just had a telephone call.'

'Was it the police again?'

'Sally, this is serious.'

Sally put down her mug. 'You're really scared, aren't you?'

'The man who called saw you drive up. He must have been watching you and staking out the cottage.' Marian finished on a choking sob. 'He said he'd be in touch again soon, then hung up.'

A steely look of determination crossed Sally's face. 'Then we'll soon see off any scumbag stalker.' She jumped to her feet.

'Sally!' Marian dragged her back down. 'What is going on?

'You tell me.'

'I know about your criminal record.' Marian blurted out her recent discovery before she could have second thoughts.

Sally sank into the depths of the sofa. 'May I ask how you found out?' she asked in a hollow voice.

'We found one of your letters to Mum in a trunk in the attic. I wasn't prying,' Marian hastened to explain. 'I thought you were in Italy when Dad had his accident.'

'That was the reason given out to explain my absence,' Sally admitted, a wry smile steadying her quivering lips.

'It wasn't true?'

'It wasn't true,' she agreed. 'To our parents what happened to me was as bad, probably worse, than having an illegitimate baby.'

Marian spluttered into her coffee.

'Put that mug down before you drench the carpet,' Sally ordered. Marian complied.

'Is that why you're being black-mailed? Because of your past?'

Sally gave a long sigh. 'I'd better tell you the whole story.' She gave a shaky smile. 'But first I am going to take a quick look outside. I'm in the right frame of mind to deal with a stalker.'

'No, don't, not now.'

'You're probably right,' Sally agreed. 'There's no point in looking for fresh trouble. Did you tell Georges of your discovery?'

Marian shook her head. 'Does Ian know?' she asked.

'You may as well know Ian and I had a huge row before I left home.'

'Another one?' Marian remained unmoved by this piece of news. 'You're always having stimulating disagreements.'

'This one was different.'

'How different?'

'I had intended confessing everything to Ian, but he's got problems at work and somehow we wound up having a major difference of opinion, and I walked out. That's why I made an appointment to meet David Hicks here.'

'I'm sorry, I don't follow.'

'I was going to tell him he could do his worst because it didn't matter anymore.'

'Who is David Hicks?'

'He was one of the gang.'

'What gang?'

'I told you it was complicated.' Sally's smile faltered. 'You were studying for your music degree in Germany, that's why you didn't know anything about what happened, but while you were abroad I got in with a bad crowd. We'd go out of a Friday evening and I often didn't get home again for the rest of the weekend. I'm ashamed now of how I behaved. Mum and Dad must have been so worried about me.'

'They never breathed a word.'

'It's not something I'm proud of, but you know me. I've always been one for thrills and spills. Life in sleepy Suffolk didn't provide enough stimulation. A group of us would go off racketing around the countryside looking for adventure. One night we wound up at a huge country house on a private estate. The gates were open so we drove in. I'm not sure whose idea it was to break into the house or to whom it belonged. Anyway, we had a bit of a party; you know, music and drink and the rest of it. It was only when the police arrived that I realised someone had reported us and that we were in serious trouble.'

'Go on,' Marian urged.

'Until then I'd assumed we had permission to be on the premises. The bedrooms had been ransacked and some expensive jewellery was found to be missing. That was the first I knew of the burglary. When the police searched my bag they discovered a diamond brooch, a necklace and some matching earrings, together with a wad of cash.'

'Sally.' Marian's mouth fell open in shock as she listened to her sister's story.

'I'm not a thief,' Sally said in a quiet voice.

'Didn't you tell the police you were innocent?'

'I tried to, but there was a lot of other stuff going on at the party. It was pretty chaotic. Someone must have panicked when the police arrived and stashed the jewellery and money in my bag. I never found out who it was.'

'You were framed.'

'To cut a long story short we were all bundled into police cars, taken down the station and charged. As I was found to be in possession of stolen property, the authorities came down heavily on me. Some of the others had influential parents and got off lightly. One or two of the gang had even run off when the police arrived. They found drugs on the premises and, well, I had a lot of money in my bag. The authorities needed to make an example of someone and unfortunately that someone was me.'

'Why?'

Sally sipped her coffee. 'There was an accident.'

'What happened?' Marian asked, aghast.

'The police found a body in one of the rooms and an empty glass by the side of the bed.'

'Who was it?'

'A girl I knew vaguely. She was a bit neurotic and I think she made a call for help, but it went wrong. Because of the raid, no one got to her in time. To make matters worse, she and I had an argument over a boy earlier in the evening. We both fancied him. I threatened to kill her.'

'None of that makes you guilty of anything.'

'I know, but I was charged with all sorts of things and, well, you know the rest.' Sally's eyes hardened at the memory.

'And David Hicks — was he involved?'

'He was charged too. He'd had a relationship with the girl in the past and as he didn't have influential parents either, to get him off the charge like me, he paid the price. We were the scapegoats and I suppose it left us both feeling very bitter. As you can imagine, I cut all contact with the others and I've never seen or heard from them since — and I don't want to. When Dad had his accident and it was obvious he would need nursing help, I gained an early release on compassionate grounds. I came home. I met Ian and the rest is history. I thought I'd managed to put my past behind me.'

'How did David find you?'

'I don't know,' Sally admitted. 'I have been heavily involved in a golf club fundraiser. He may have read about me in the local newspaper. They did a double-page spread on the club and my photo was in it. It wouldn't have been too difficult for him to get my number from the organisers. He probably posed as a donor or something like that. He first contacted me about six months ago. We met up and I felt sorry for him.

He hasn't done well in life so I gave him some money to help him on his way. I thought that would be the last I would see of him, but a few weeks later he turned up at the house demanding another larger payment, this time for his silence.'

'You didn't give in to him?'

'What else could I do? Ian's mother suffers badly with her nerves and any hint of a scandal could have serious repercussions on her health. Then there are the children to consider. No one wants to learn their mother has a criminal record.'

'Why did you suggest meeting David here?'

'I'm not coming out of this very well, am I?' Sally's smile wasn't quite so confident as she admitted, 'I didn't want David visiting my house and finding me on my own. I suggested he come up here. I thought between the three of us — that's you, Georges and me — we could see him off if he turned nasty. I shouldn't have involved you, I know, but I'm at my wits' end. The only way to see this thing through is to tell Ian, but I can't now because I don't know when I'm ever going to see him again.'

'You poor thing.' Marian squeezed Sally's fingers.

'You don't know the half of it,' Sally admitted.

'Why didn't you tell me before now?'

'I was too ashamed to. You were always a goody two-shoes. Mum and Dad kept comparing me to you, unfavourably.'

'That's not true.'

'Maybe not, but that's how I saw it. Anyway, last night after I blurted out that I was being blackmailed, I got cold feet. When you rang this morning I didn't know what to do, before I realised panicking wasn't the answer and it was time to face up to things. Besides, it's not fair to involve you in my sordid past. So I jumped in the car, drove hell for leather across the country, and here I am. Please say you still love me, warts and all.'

'Sisters are there for each other, you know.' Marian hugged her. 'I'm not about to disown you.'

There was the suspicion of moisture in Sally's green eyes as she dabbed at them with a tissue. 'We've never been that close, have we, after that business with Ian? I mean, he was your date and I pinched him from you. You don't know how I've suffered for the way I behaved that night. It's just that I saw him as a way out of the nightmare that had been my life. He was respectable — had prospects, wealthy parents.' She shrugged. 'Sometimes I hate myself.'

'There's no need to go into all that now,' Marian brushed aside her confession. 'You've been married for years and I'm engaged to Georges, so let's let bygones be bygones.'

'That's as maybe.' There was a trace of the old Sally back as she vowed, 'But I'm not having David Hicks frightening the life out of you. I can't imagine how he got hold of this number. I didn't give it to him.'

'Do you think it was his jacket the police found on the beach?'

'I've no idea, but what I don't understand is why he was loitering about outside. Why didn't he simply knock on the door, rather than make a threatening telephone call to you? It doesn't make sense.'

'I don't think the mystery caller was David Hicks,' Marian admitted.

'If it wasn't him then who was it?' Sally demanded.

After a short pause, Marian admitted, 'I think it was my son.'

7

The weak January sun was setting over the harbour as Marian drove into the coastal fishing village. The boats had been pulled up and secured for the day and the harbour front was deserted. No snow had fallen in this part of the country and although Marian's journey had been a long one, she had started well before daybreak and she hadn't been unduly troubled by the weather. The roads were quiet and the cross-country drive had been relatively easy.

How Sally had persuaded her into setting off on her quest, Marian still didn't understand. Her sister had always been strong-willed and Marian now understood why. Life hadn't dealt her the kindest of hands.

Once Marian had confessed her story about Peter and Valentin, Sally had leapt into action. 'What a pair we are.

Honestly, talk about family secrets.' Sally hugged her. 'What you must have gone through. Promise me no matter what goes wrong in future, you come to me, you hear?'

'Same goes here,' Marian agreed, a sob catching the back of her throat. The relief of confessing her past to Sally was a weight off her mind.

'The Barr sisters rule, OK?'

Sally raised her palm and Marian slapped hers against it.

'Now,' Sally said, getting down to business, 'first we need to confront the lion in his den.'

'We what?'

'You need to track down your stalker and find out if he really is your son sending these letters and making horrible telephone calls.'

'He might still be outside.'

Sally shook her head. 'He's gone. I feel it in my bones. Probably knew he couldn't take on the two of us. So we'd better start now.'

'I can't.'

' 'Can't' is a negative word. We do not use negative words,' Sally lectured Marian with a stern frown.

'I mean we can't because adoption details are confidential.'

'Rot.'

'The law is the law. It's done to protect the privacy of all parties.'

'There must be a file somewhere.'

'I expect there is, but we won't be given access to it.'

Sally chewed the top of one of her new pencils as she made notes. 'Where was Peter born?' she asked, after thinking things through.

'Guildford, in Surrey.'

'What were you doing there?'

'Attending a music seminar. He was born two weeks early. That's why Valentin was driving late at night. He was coming to see us.' Marian's voice gave out on her as she recalled the fateful night of his accident.

Sally clutched her hand. 'Sorry, I didn't mean to upset you by raking up your past.'

'You didn't. Seventeen years is a long time ago. I have moved on.'

'Do you want to go on with this?' Sally asked.

Marian hesitated. 'I wouldn't want to upset Peter's adoptive mother, and if it isn't Peter making a nuisance of himself then we could be stirring up a hornet's nest.'

'I agree, but we need to get to the bottom of what's happening.'

'What about David Hicks? Isn't he a bigger threat? He also knows this address and the telephone number. He could appear at any moment and start demanding money from you.'

Sally batted away Marian's question as if it were no more than a fly making a minor nuisance of itself. 'If my marriage to Ian is going to stand a chance, I'm going to have to confess all. I don't want any secrets between us. I think that's why I was so ready to argue with him. I felt guilty, but I've had enough of the guilt-trip thing. I've decided if and when we do get back together I'll tell Ian everything.'

'And if David gets to him first?'

'Why should he want to kill the goose that lays the golden egg?'

'You never know.'

'Then he will have done my job for me, won't he?' It was Sally's smile that was now shaky. 'You did promise to stick by me, didn't you?' There was an earnest look on her face as she asked her question.

'Through thick and thin,' Marian assured her.

'Right then, back to business, and no more negative talk. Where did you stay after Peter was born?'

'In a small home run by the church. I was in a mess emotionally and I needed to sort myself out. They were very kind to me and we were given little jobs to do to pay our way. I worked in the laundry. Others tended the garden, some did the cooking.'

'Were all the babies put up for adoption?'

Marian shook her head. 'There was

no pressure. Some families had second thoughts and took their daughters home, but for those who didn't have any support discreet arrangements were made. There was a small team of nursing and administrative staff on hand to see to everything.'

'You didn't by any chance keep this anonymous letter that followed you half way around the world?' Sally enquired after a few more moments of deep thought.

'Devon.' Marian sat up straight.

'I beg your pardon?' Sally stopped chewing her pencil.

'Or it might have been Dorset.'

'What are we talking about now?' Sally asked.

'I told you about the nurse who let me slip that duck into Peter's cot blanket?'

'Yes, but you didn't mention Devon.'

'She did. She said . . . ' Marian screwed up her eyes in concentration as she tried to recall the details. ' . . . The West Country was a lovely part of the world because that was where she came from too, and Peter was a very lucky baby to be going to live there.'

'Then half our problem is solved,' Sally crowed. 'Now all we need to do is find out the name of the people who adopted him and we're home and dry. I suppose you don't have any ideas on that one?'

'It could be Bartholomew,' Marian admitted with a slow nod.

'How did you work that one out?'

'It was something another nurse let slip. Two of them were talking outside my door. They thought I was asleep, but I wasn't, and I heard what they were saying. I used my maiden name at the home because Valentin's surname was so difficult to spell. One said changing Peter's name from Barr to Bartholomew wouldn't require much paperwork as the first three letters of his new surname were the same.'

'Well God bless your big ears,' Sally laughed. 'We've got Devon.' She ticked the items off on her fingers. 'And Bartholomew.'

'It's not a lot to go on.'

'All we've got to do is run a check through the computer. That won't be a problem. We shouldn't have any trouble tracking down Peter's family.'

Marian did not share her sister's optimism. 'It was seventeen years ago. People move. Things change.'

'Can you come up with a better idea?'

Marian had to admit she couldn't.

'Then let's get cracking.'

'What do we do,' Marian asked, 'if we do find something?'

'You go down there.'

'I can't hare off to the West Country on a whim.'

'Why not? And it's not a whim.'

'Maybe not, but it will probably be a wild goose chase.'

'You need to know if this person really is Peter, or someone out to cause trouble.'

'I could contact the police,' Marian suggested.

'And tell them what? That you

received a crank anonymous letter, months after it was written, and which you have now destroyed? You found a plastic duck on the floor of a barn and someone telephoned you pretending to be the son you'd given up for adoption seventeen years ago? I don't actually think they'd give it top priority.'

'He didn't say he was my son. He only asked if the name Peter meant anything to me.'

'Whatever, it's not a lot for the police to go on is it?'

'I suppose not.'

'Look, you've arranged your professional schedule to include some time off. Georges has been called away to Salzburg. I can deal with things here. You're a free agent.'

'There's the charity gala committee meeting. I said I'd take Georges' place. One of us ought to attend.'

'I can speak to the organisers on your behalf. If there's one thing I know all about at the moment, it's charity fundraisers. Marian, you need to put your mind at rest and you won't get a better chance.'

'I don't like to leave you here on your own.'

'It would only be for a day or two.'

'Supposing David Hicks comes looking for you when I'm not here?'

'I can deal with him,' Sally insisted. 'Now,' she said, dragging her laptop out of its case, 'let's get looking for the Bartholomews of deepest Devon. Do you have anything else to go on?'

'I seem to have it at the back of my mind that Peter's new home was on the Dorset border.'

'Right. Let's see what we can find.'

Sally identified several possibilities by means of making one or two telephone calls and pretending to conduct a customer survey. Marian was astounded by her sister's ingenuity when the list was narrowed down to a small fishing village on the Jurassic Coast. To both the sisters' surprise, a Mrs Peggy Bartholomew ran a boarding establishment for summer visitors and had lived in the area for over twenty years.

'I usually close up during the winter months,' she explained to Sally over the telephone, 'but we had a quiet summer and I need the business so this year I decided to stay open. I have vacancies, so your sister would be welcome to stay.'

'Off you go,' Sally had instructed her, 'and good luck.'

★　★　★

The Red House was situated inland from the harbour and boasted a small parking space for visitors on the outside forecourt. On the pretext of needing a few days' peace and quiet from her hectic professional schedule, Sally had booked Marian in. How she was going to approach the delicate subject of adoption, she didn't know, but she'd come too far to back out now.

'Welcome.' Mrs Bartholomew stood on the step and greeted Marian as she unloaded her suitcase from the car.

'Miss Barr, isn't it? You'll be the only guest so I've put you in the front room, a nice double overlooking the sea — well, not quite, but on a clear day you can see out a long way.' She was a plump middle-aged woman, and Marian found herself hoping she was the Mrs Bartholomew she was looking for.

'I don't normally provide dinner for my guests, but to be honest tonight I'd be glad of the company. My boy was supposed to visit over the weekend but he's been held up due to all the bad weather. There's a backlog at work and he has to catch up. Goodness knows when I'll be seeing him, so I'm all on my own.'

'What about your husband?' Marian asked.

'I'm a widow. Now, could you manage a bit of fish stew? Your sister says you're a concert pianist?' Still chatting away, Mrs Bartholomew relieved Marian of her suitcase and carried it up the stairs. 'I've a pot of tea on the go; shall I bring you up a tray? I expect you're ready for some refreshment after your long journey.'

The room was basic but neat and clean.

'There isn't much to do of a winter's day,' Mrs Bartholomew admitted when she delivered the loaded tray to Marian's room, 'so I like to keep the place looking nice. Call me Peggy by the way,' she invited. 'And you are?'

'Marian.'

'Have we met before?' Peggy asked, looking into her eyes.

'I don't think so,' Marian answered, ignoring the twinge of unease creeping up her spine.

'Funny, I could have sworn I've seen you somewhere. Anyway, I'll leave you to settle in. Don't let your tea get cold.'

Marian stretched out on the bed after Peggy left. Her eyes felt heavy from the strain of the past few days, and within moments she fell fast asleep.

She was in the middle of a concert. She had forgotten where she was or what particular piece she was supposed to be playing. The conductor was tapping his baton urgently on his music stand to attract her attention. Marian jerked awake as the tapping grew more insistent. Clutching a pillow, she looked round the room in puzzled confusion.

'Marian? Sorry to disturb you.' Peggy poked her head round the door. 'Only, I was worried. It's gone seven and I wanted to check everything's all right.'

Marian stifled a yawn behind the back of her hand. 'I fell asleep.' She blinked at the clock. 'Goodness, is that the time?'

'The coastal air does that to folk. You were more than ready for a break, I'd say. Shall I pull your curtains and switch on the light?'

Marian swung her legs over the side of the bed and stretched her aching limbs.

'The bathroom is down the end of the hall if you want to freshen up.

Would supper in half an hour suit you?'

'Thank you.' Marian picked up her sponge bag and padded down the corridor. She looked at her reflection in the mirror. Two nights' lack of sleep was already having an effect on her complexion, and her hair looked dull and listless. She would have liked to take a shower but there wasn't time. Running a bowl of hot water, she did her best to repair the damage of the journey.

As she turned off the taps, her sponge bag fell off the cramped shelf above the washbasin and onto the floor. The impact dislodged the vanity unit mirror and it swung open, revealing an array of personal toiletries. As Marian closed the door she noticed a razor, some male cologne and a shaving brush. Her hand trembled as she reached out to touch them. Were they Peter's? Peggy mentioned that she was a widow, so they couldn't belong to her husband. Marian stroked the hairs of the shaving brush, closing her eyes when the pain became too much to bear.

She didn't possess a sixth sense, but something was telling her Peggy was the woman who had adopted her son.

8

Peggy was speaking on the telephone in the hall when Marian descended the stairs. She turned a worried face to greet her as she hurriedly finished her call. 'There you are.' She did her best to smile but Marian could see she was troubled. 'Come on through. We'll eat in the kitchen, if that's all right with you? It's cosier on winter nights. I don't often use the dining room this time of year.'

The herbal smell of a stew simmering in the oven greeted Marian as Peggy pushed open the door. 'Something smells good,' Marian said, sniffing.

'Lovely isn't it?' Peggy's smile was slowly coming back to life. 'I never know what I'm going to cook of an evening. It all depends on the day's catch. Sometimes during the winter the fishermen don't get out if the weather's too bad, but today they came back with a fair catch of cod. I also got a razor fish — difficult to cook for most people, but very delicate flesh once you've made the effort. I added a few prawns from my freezer so there'll be more than enough for the two of us. Sit down and I'll find us something to drink.'

'What about your son?' Marian decided to start asking questions as soon as she could. 'Will he be joining us?'

'Brian?'

'Is that his name?' Marian asked in a carefully casual voice.

'That was him on the telephone.' Peggy now had her head in the fridge. 'I've some fresh orange juice.' She held up a container. 'Would that suit you?'

'Fine, thank you.'

'Help yourself to bread while I'm getting things ready,' Peggy invited, pointing to the crusty cob loaf and crock of butter on the table. 'Did you stop for any lunch?'

Marian shook her head. 'I wanted to press on.'

'And you missed your tea too,' Peggy tutted. 'It's not good to miss meals. Brian's a delivery driver and his diet appals me. He eats far too many greasy fry-ups at strange times of the day, and when he can't stop he nibbles on bars of chocolate, but I don't dare nag him. He's like his father and can be a bit short-tempered.'

'Was your husband a fisherman?' Marian asked as she spread butter on a slice of the loaf.

'Yes, out in all weathers he was.'

'Brian didn't follow in his footsteps?'

'Do you have children?' Peggy's question temporarily unsettled Marian.

'I'm not married,' she said by way of reply.

Peggy nodded, then said after a short pause, 'I expect you still know what the young are like. They need to do their own thing. Brian's been a bit of a wanderlust all his life. This part of the world was too quiet for him. He was always in trouble of some sort. First chance he could, he got a delivery job. That way he could see more of the country. It suits him fine. He's a free spirit. Doesn't take kindly to authority.' Peggy's West Country burr softened her words. 'I should love my son, I know, but he's not like me.'

'Is he stuck somewhere because of the snow?' Marian sensed undertones in their relationship. She also suspected Peggy wasn't telling her everything.

'That's what his call was about,' Peggy explained as she doled out generous portions of fish stew onto two warmed plates. 'I was expecting him to visit, but he told me he hasn't finished his rounds. You know, he sleeps in the back of that van of his too. It can't be right, but he says it's cheaper than booking a room.' She sat down opposite Marian. 'Tuck in. I made the stew to a family recipe that's been handed down over the generations. The contents are a closely guarded secret, but no one's ever turned down a second helping.'

Peggy was looking happier now and once Marian started on her supper, she realised how hungry she was.

'Knew you wouldn't be disappointed,' Peggy said as she collected their empty plates at the end of the meal. 'Are you sure you've had enough?'

'More than enough,' Marian replied.

'I've some apple pie in the fridge.'

'No really, I couldn't.'

Peggy looked disappointed. 'I'm going to have some,' she coaxed.

'A very small slice then,' Marian capitulated, and she was rewarded with a smile.

'I always say a meal isn't finished off unless there's a proper sweet.' Peggy's idea of a small slice differed wildly from Marian's, but again she did justice to the home-cooked pie and sighed in satisfaction as she cleared her plate.

'I shall need a brisk walk in the morning to work it all off,' Marian said.

'I enjoy a stroll down to the harbour when I have the time. There's plenty to see by the water's edge,' Peggy replied. 'You sit there while I do the dishes then we'll have our coffee.'

'Please,' Marian said, standing up, 'let me help.'

'A helping hand would be nice,' Peggy said, squirting washing-up liquid into the bowl. 'In a house full of men, I suppose I grew used to doing everything. You don't mind staying in the kitchen?' she asked while the coffee was percolating.

'Not at all,' Marian replied. 'You're right. It is very cosy.'

'You can tell me all about your career. I like a bit of music of an evening when I'm on my own. What sort of things do you play?'

'Concerts, operas, gala performances,' Marian explained.

'The classics? That's lovely. Do you travel all over the world?'

'Yes. It can be quite a strenuous schedule.'

'I can imagine.' Peggy's weather-beaten face creased into a happy smile.

'It must be a dream job.'

'It is.'

'At times I think I would have liked a career, but I am a bit of a home bird.'

'Have you always lived in this part of the world?' Marian asked.

'I was born in the village. My husband was an incomer. Moved down with his family from Sussex when he was a boy. He worked on the boats with my father. That's how we met. He was the only boyfriend I ever had. Pat played the field a bit with some of the local girls, but I saw them all off. I told him if we were going to settle down I needed to know where I stood.'

'You proposed to him?' Marian asked, raising her eyebrows in surprise.

'In not so many words, I suppose I did,' Peggy admitted. 'I can be quite straightforward at times. I knew Pat was the one for me and I didn't see the point in bothering with other men. Course he tried to wriggle a bit; what man doesn't? I had a word with my father, who told him flat there wasn't a job for him if he didn't knuckle down and get a wife and start a family.'

'I think these days that sort of behaviour could be classed as harassment.'

'Call it what you like,' Peggy chuckled. 'It worked. We had a long and happy marriage until I lost him last winter.'

'That must have been a sad time for you.'

'I coped. I had my Brian.' She paused. 'Even if at times he has caused me heartache.'

'Is he your only child?' Marian asked.

The kitchen fell silent. The ticking of the clock grew louder as Peggy didn't reply. 'He is now,' she eventually admitted.

To cover her embarrassment, Marian nibbled on an almond biscuit she didn't really want.

'I had two sons.' Peggy's voice was now so soft, Marian had to lean forward to hear what she was saying. 'Brian and Peter.'

The remains of Marian's biscuit fell into her coffee but neither of them noticed.

'Peter was eight years younger than Brian.'

'Was?' Marian had difficulty finding her voice.

'He died,' Peggy replied with a look of intense sadness on her face.

Marian bit down a cry of shock. 'No,' she gasped, unable to conceal her grief.

'It's true I'm afraid. Would you like a glass of water?'

Marian was breathing heavily. Peggy rose and filled a tumbler with tap water. 'You're his mother, aren't you?' she said, the keen brown eyes never leaving Marian's face.

Marian gulped down some water. Its coolness eased the ache in her throat. 'I gave birth to a son seventeen years ago,' she admitted.

'I knew it from the moment I saw you,' Peggy replied. 'He had your eyes.'

'What — I mean how — did he die?'

'In a car accident. My husband never

really got over the shock. He wasn't a strong man. It's a hard life on the water, but after Peter's death he seemed to fade. I watched him get thinner by the day. The accident robbed me of two of the people I loved most in this world.'

'I'm so very sorry.' Marian wanted to take Peggy in her arms and comfort her for her losses. She was more of a mother to Peter than Marian had ever been, and she could only imagine the pain his loss must have caused her.

'I can't really talk about it.' Peggy sounded so sad it tore into Marian's soul.

It had been a pointless idea to come all the way down here on a whim. There was no way she could tell this heartbroken woman that she suspected her other son Brian might be the one threatening her. It would only lead to more heartbreak, and Peggy Bartholomew had been through enough.

'I understand.'

'Will you be staying on, now you've

got what you came for?' Peggy asked.

Marian flinched at the harsh tone of her voice. 'I don't know.'

'I should warn you, my Brian doesn't take to strangers. He was jealous of Peter. He hated to share.'

'He hasn't threatened you?' Marian asked.

'He didn't while my husband was alive, but now . . . well, I'm thinking of putting the house up for sale. It's too much work for me on my own and Brian needs the money.'

The more Marian heard about Brian, the more she began to dislike him.

'When I told him I had a guest booked in for this evening, he was quite annoyed. He suggested I ask you to leave.'

'Did you tell him my name?'

'No.' Peggy looked surprised by the question. 'But it wouldn't have made any difference if I had, would it?'

'I suppose not. But now you know who I am, would you like me to leave?' Marian asked.

Peggy frowned. 'How did you find

out about me? I thought adoption details were confidential.'

'No one broke the trust,' Marian assured her. 'My sister and I indulged in a bit of amateur sleuthing.'

'Peter wanted to find you, you know. It started off as a school project. They were doing research into family trees and he asked me if I would mind if he tried to trace you. We always told him from the very beginning that he was adopted. We said he was specially chosen. Brian didn't like that very much.'

'Is that why Brian was jealous?'

'He was an only child for so long. When it was obvious I wasn't going to have another baby, Pat and I decided to adopt. From the moment we told Brian he began to be difficult, but you mustn't think Peter had a sad life; he was a very happy boy. He inherited your love of music. He loved to sing.'

'His father was a tenor,' Marian admitted. 'We were actually married.'

'You don't have to explain,' Peggy insisted.

'I'd like to.'

'Not tonight. You're too tired. We've both had a bit of a shock I'd say.'

'As you wish,' Marian agreed.

'One thing I have to say, Marian.' Peggy began heating up some water. 'I always put bottles in the bed at night,' she explained, concentrating on her task before she spoke again. 'I don't want to know the reasons why you gave up your son. It's none of my business but I knew you must have loved him very much when I found that little plastic duck in his blanket and read the words you had carved in the base. We used to play with it in the bath and I told him it was a present from his other mother.' Peggy's eyes were moist as she went on. 'I'm not much of a one for words but thank you for giving him to me.' She began ferociously twisting the top of the filled hot water bottle before thrusting it into Marian's hands. 'He was very like you and I know you would have been proud of him. Now off you go upstairs to bed.'

Peggy thrust Marian towards the stairs before she could speak. Up in her room with her heart still beating rapidly, Marian dialled Sally's number. It rang out. Marian glanced at her watch. Sally was a night bird. She wouldn't be in bed yet. The call switched to voicemail.

'Sally?' Marian cleared her throat. It was still clogged with emotion. 'Look, I've too much to tell you over the telephone. I'll be home as soon as I can. Love you.'

When Marian awoke the next morning after a dreamless sleep, she found a note from Peggy under her door.

''I had to go out,'' Marian read. ''Make yourself some breakfast. I thought perhaps you would like the enclosed as a keepsake.''

A photograph fluttered to the ground. Marian picked it up. It was of a young boy smiling confidently into the camera. On the back was written the name Peter.

9

There was no sign of Sally at Hatpin Cottage when an exhausted Marian staggered through the door. Two long drives in such a short space of time was too much for anyone, she thought as she flung her car keys onto the telephone table.

She knew she had no one to blame but herself. Besides, she needed to feel tired; she needed not to think about Peter. She needed complete rest.

She pushed open the sitting room door. Sally had left things in a huge mess. Boxes were strewn everywhere and letters had been discarded, as if read in a hurry and then dropped to the floor without a second thought. True to form, Sally had arrived, stirred everything up, and then left without a word of where she was going. So much for her resolution of being a good sister,

Marian thought.

She stooped down to pick up a packet of pencils off the carpet and ran her finger over Sally's name embossed at the top in gold lettering. She had been childishly proud of them. Marian was surprised she hadn't bothered to take them with her.

She sat down and rested her head in her hands. For the moment she was too tired to work anything out but all she knew was Peter, her son, hadn't been responsible for the threatening telephone call or the anonymous letter she had received, nor could he have dropped the yellow plastic duck on the floor of the deserted barn.

After Georges had departed for Salzburg, Marian had hidden the duck away in the bottom of her music case where no one would find it. There had been too much going on for her to examine it properly. Some time she would need to get it out again to see if it could provide any clues.

Her mobile vibrated. Marian half

decided not to answer it; then, knowing she would only worry if she didn't, she retrieved it from her bag.

'Mrs Wren?' She identified Georges' personal assistant as the caller. 'Is anything wrong?'

'Miss Barr?' She sounded anxious as she asked, 'Is Mr Pascal with you?'

'No, he's in Salzburg.'

'He isn't. I've had an irate telephone call from Richard Walton. His agent is most annoyed. Apparently Mr Pascal has broken his contract.'

'He's done what?' Marian sat up straight on the sofa.

'He walked out in the middle of rehearsals without a word to anyone. Mr Walton doesn't know where he's gone.'

'Georges would never do anything so unprofessional. When did all this happen?'

'I'm not sure. Are you still at your parents' cottage?'

'Yes, I stayed on after Georges was called away.'

'And you've been there all the time?'

Marian cleared her throat. 'Actually no, I haven't.'

'You haven't?' Mrs Wren was quick to pick up on the hesitation.

'I had some private business to attend to.'

'Perhaps Mr Pascal has been trying to contact you at the cottage. Was it unoccupied during this time?'

'My sister was here.'

'And is she still there?'

'No, she isn't.'

'Do you know where she is?'

'No, I don't. I'd better speak to Georges' agent,' Marian decided.

'I would be most grateful if you would. He's such a terse man I could barely get a word in edgewise.'

Marian trawled through her messages received. There were none from Georges or Sally. Surely they couldn't have met up at the cottage and gone off together? Marian instantly quelled the thought. They hadn't ever met, but supposing Georges had returned for some reason and found Sally here?

Given Sally's history, Marian hoped her suspicions about her sister were unfounded. Sally had been married to Ian for years and although it probably wasn't the perfect union, they had reached an understanding. Marian didn't give much credence to Sally's story about a trial separation. She was sure they would get back together; and until they did, she hoped Sally would be faithful to her husband.

Where did that leave Georges? He suspected she was hiding something from him. Did he truly think she had a lover? Was he bent on revenge for what he perceived as her unfaithfulness? Would Sally be the answer to his revenge? She was an attractive woman and by her own admittance there had been one or two affairs. Ian travelled a lot and Sally didn't like being on her own.

How had her life got into such a complicated mess? What was supposed to have been a peaceful Fenland break was turning into a nightmare, with calls from the police, blackmail, shadows from her past coming back to haunt her — and now Georges had disappeared. She dialled Richard Walton's number.

'Was he under any pressure?' He fired the question at Marian before she had a chance to speak.

'No.'

'You haven't had a disagreement?'

'Georges was annoyed to be called away at such short notice but he is professional enough to realise that's the nature of his work. What happened, exactly, in Salzburg?'

'I got a message saying he hadn't turned up for rehearsals. The hotel weren't even aware he had checked out.'

'Have you telephoned the airlines?'

'They won't give out details over the telephone. Mrs Wren knows nothing. I wish my artists wouldn't do this. It places me in a very difficult situation. I thought Georges had outgrown this type of behaviour.'

Richard ended the call before Marian had a chance to suggest he contact the police.

She dialled Sally's number, but again was diverted to voice mail. She knew from personal experience that her sister could be anywhere. It wasn't unknown for her to fly off to Verbier on a whim.

Marian leaned back against the squashy sofa cushions and closed her eyes. It was at times like this when she missed the calming presence of her mother. Over the years they had grown closer, and Marian had been touched to discover an album among her personal effects. Every newspaper cutting and review of her performances had been painstakingly pasted into it, together with photos of her daughter receiving various awards. Her mother belonged to a generation that didn't show open emotions as easily as their children, but her pride in her daughter's achievements was obvious from the way she had dated and noted the cuttings.

Marian's head fell forward. Her eyes

felt too heavy to stay open. She would sort something out, but right now she was too tired to think straight.

The glass of the window shattered as someone threw a brick through it. Marian screamed. Shards of splintered glass littered the carpet. A face appeared at the window.

'Open the door,' Georges yelled, 'before I break all the windows!'

Teeth chattering with shock, Marian ran into the hall.

'Hurry up,' Georges bellowed from the other side.

'It's stiff,' Marian sobbed as several of her fingernails broke under the pressure.

The door finally gave way and the next moment she was enveloped in Georges' arms. His heart was a double drumbeat against hers. He began to frantically kiss her.

'Georges.' Marian's attempts to push him away had no effect. The urgency of his embrace was nothing like she had ever known before. Her body was aflame from the pressure of his lips on her flesh. 'What is going on? Everyone's looking for you — Mrs Wren, Richard . . . '

He gasped as his eyes devoured hers. 'Where is he?' he demanded.

'Where's who?'

'Your lover.'

Marian was forced to cling onto Georges to stop herself from toppling over. 'I don't have a lover.'

'Then why did that man ring me and tell me you were together?'

'What man?'

Georges' blue eyes burned into Marian's. 'I chartered a private jet and paid the pilot double the fee to get me back here. Marian, I love you. Don't do this to me.' He hugged Marian so hard he squeezed the breath out of her lungs.

Perspiration dripped from his brow onto her face. The room swayed as Marian began to feel dizzy from the strength of his passionate embrace.

'Georges, there's no need to crush the life out of me.'

'Then you'd better tell me what this is all about. When I find him I will kill him.'

'There's no need to kill anyone, Georges. Calm down.'

'I let you fob me off the other night, but it won't work a second time. There's another man in your life, isn't there?'

'No,' Marian insisted, 'there isn't.'

'Don't you understand how much I love you?'

Marian laid her head against his shoulder. She could feel the pulse in his neck beating against her cheek.

'Before you tell me how much you love me there is something I have to tell you,' she said in a quiet voice.

'I was right. You don't love me.'

'I do.'

'Then there is another man in your life?'

Marian took a deep breath. 'Yes.'

Georges' eyes glittered like shards of blue ice. 'I would never have believed it.' His fingertips dug into her flesh, his voice full of anguish.

'There are two.'

'How can you be so cruel?'

'I've been married before and I have — I had — a son.'

* * *

'You should have trusted me.' Georges still didn't look entirely convinced after Marian finished her confession. 'For that I will never forgive you.'

Marian feared her shoulders would be permanently bruised from the pressure of his fingertips on her shoulders.

'I wanted to, but you put me on a pedestal. Georges, I'm not perfect. I have a past.'

'Not such a very terrible past.' He kissed her eyelids. 'Although for you it must have been very bad. My poor darling, what you have been through . . . But you need not worry now. I am not about to desert you because of this Valentin, although I am prepared to hate the very mention of his name.'

124

The coal fire burned in the newly swept grate. Between them they managed to board up the broken window and tidy up the mess on the floor. After several animated telephone calls, Georges had assured Richard he would be back in Salzburg in time for the dress rehearsal.

'My agent is convinced all this is your fault,' Georges informed Marian, a wicked twinkle in his eyes, 'and I agreed with him.'

'That's not fair,' Marian protested.

'Fair or not, you can see the effect you have on me.' Georges tightened his hold around Marian's shoulders. 'Never would I have thought I would do such a thing. Until now my music has been my life, but the idea of you in another man's arms turned me insane.'

'That's why I didn't tell you about my past.' Marian sagged against him in relief. 'I was scared what you might do.'

'You are right. I could not think straight. I was mad with rage.'

'Why didn't you simply telephone me?'

'I wanted to confront you in person with this lover.'

'I hope you weren't thinking of challenging him to a duel,' Marian laughed, then immediately regretted her suggestion as Georges seemed to take it seriously.

'That I had not thought of. It is a good idea. Somewhere I have an antique duelling pistol.'

'No,' Marian insisted.

'Perhaps you're right,' Georges agreed. 'My aim isn't very good.'

'What are we going to do now?' Marian hastily changed the subject.

'Tell me about this Brian.'

'I don't know that it is him causing trouble,' she put in quickly, 'or that he was the person who rang you.'

'But you suspect it might be him?'

'I can't think of anyone else, and his mother said he was jealous of Peter.'

'Jealousy is an emotion I understand. It makes people do strange things. But why has he waited until now to cause trouble? Why did he telephone me? Was it for money?'

'Peter was charting his family tree. Brian could have seen his notes. I don't know.' Marian shrugged. 'There could be lots of reasons.'

'Whatever, you are not safe here. Come back to Salzburg with me.'

'I won't do that,' Marian protested.

'Why not?'

'I refuse to be hounded out of my home by a screwball who thinks he can scare me, and nothing you can say will persuade me to change my mind.'

Georges' eyes softened. 'I suspected you would say something like that. You are the perfect English rose, but like the rose you have sharp thorns.'

Marian rested her head on Georges' chest. She could feel the strength of his muscles against the side of her neck. Her eyelids drooped from the relief of knowing there were no further secrets between them.

'We mustn't forget the charity concert committee in all this,' she murmured sleepily. 'Sally was going to speak to the chair for me but it looks like that's something else she has overlooked.'

'This sister of yours,' Georges began.

'Yes?'

'You don't think she is involved in all this funny business?'

'Sally?' Marian shook her head.

'That man she was due to meet here, the one who did not turn up? What was all that about?'

Marian had kept quiet about Sally's past. That was a part of the story Georges did not need to know yet. If Sally decided to go public then it was her own business, but until she had confessed all to Ian, her husband, Marian didn't feel it was right for her to tell Georges. She'd seen firsthand how he could over-react to a potentially threatening situation.

'Sally does get involved in things,' Marian admitted, 'but she wouldn't do anything to harm me — us.'

'But you do not know where she is?'

'She'll turn up again in time.'

'Has she done this sort of thing before?'

'Occasionally.'

'Well, if you are not going to come to Salzburg with me, where are you going to go?'

'Back to London. I have things I need to catch up on. Then Paris?'

'Of course.' Georges leaned forward and sipped his wine, then half turned to Marian and with a lazy smile said, 'But for the moment we have some other business to see to.'

There was no mistaking his meaning. The flames from the fire reflected the passion in his eyes. 'I have proved to you how much I love you,' he said simply. 'Now it is your turn to return the compliment.'

10

Sally had never visited this part of Essex before. Business parks in any part of the country weren't exactly her scene. She tapped the steering wheel with her gloved hands. She was feeling rather pleased with herself. Private detective work wasn't that difficult if you knew what you were doing, and she owed it to Marian to help her sort out her personal life.

Stealing Ian from her sister had weighed heavily on her conscience for years, and now there was the very real threat of another of Marian's relationships hitting the rocks. Sally gave a tense nod of her head. That must not be allowed to happen.

Sally hadn't wanted to scare Marian, but she had spotted a white delivery van parked near Hatpin Cottage when she arrived. It had looked so out of place that as she had driven by, she made a mental note of the telephone number painted on the side panel. When she had looked out of the window later it had gone.

With her suspicions aroused, as soon as Marian left for the West Country Sally did a quick trawl of the internet. It wasn't long before her searches revealed the location of the van's area code. Tapping one of her new pencils against her teeth, she debated what to do. She had never been one to sit still and as the snow was beginning to thaw, there was nothing to stop her carrying out a little research. She would never get a better chance than this.

There had been no word from Ian and Sally still wasn't sure how things stood between them, but the girls were at school; and since she could contact them any time she chose, for the moment there was no reason to go home to an empty house. Sally decided to track down the lowlife who was upsetting her sister. She would tell him to get a life of his own, even if he turned out to be Marian's long-lost son.

Without a second glance at the chaos on the sitting room floor, or considering the danger in which she was being placed, Sally had jumped into her car and driven off. During a comfort break at a services area she had dialled the telephone number on the side of the van. The girl who answered sounded friendly and helpful. Emboldened, Sally asked if any of their drivers had been in the Suffolk area during the last few days. Her question was met with a suspicious silence and she realised in her enthusiasm for information she might have overstepped the mark.

'Why do you want to know?' the operator eventually asked.

'No reason,' Sally laughed off the question. 'I was up there myself, stranded in the snow,' she said, thinking on her feet, 'and I caught sight of one of your vehicles. I'm clearing out my parents' cottage,' she improvised, 'and I wondered if your operatives undertook work in the area.'

'I see.' The tone of the girl's voice softened. 'Well we don't actually do removal work as such. We're a delivery company.'

'Where are you based?' Sally asked. Really, this was too easy, she thought as the girl gave her the exact location of the unit.

The Railway Approach was a converted block of old Victorian warehouses that looked as though it had fallen into disuse until someone appeared to have had the bright idea of using it for business purposes. As Sally watched, several vehicles all with different business logos trundled in and out of the large iron railing gates.

One of the drivers gave her a cheery wave and tooted his horn. Sally ducked. She didn't want to draw attention to her presence. Now she was here she wasn't exactly sure what she was going to do. Another blast on a horn made her jump. A gesticulating driver urged her forward. She was blocking the entrance. Sally had no choice but to drive into the forecourt and park. She could see a female in reception answering the switchboard. Taking a deep breath, Sally turned off her engine and headed towards the office.

★   ★   ★

Brian flicked off the control switch and leaned back in his swivel chair. He'd always had the gift of the gab and the boss had totally swallowed his story about giving a member of the public a lift in the van, although it was strictly against company rules, because she was a little old lady lost in the snow. The last bit was actually true, although he had only decided to offer her a lift when he realised where she lived. Another stroke of luck had been when she left her copy of the local newspaper in his van and he read about Marian Barr's imminent visit — better and better.

'That's why I was delayed,' he

finished explaining to his boss, 'and why I was a bit off course. I mean it wouldn't have looked good, would it, boss? Leaving her alone at the bus stop with her weekly shopping? No one had any idea when the next bus was due. It probably hasn't even turned up yet.'

'Don't make a habit of it,' his boss growled in reply. 'Now you are here,' he continued, 'I have to go out. I'll need you to operate the control board in my absence.'

'Fine,' Brian readily agreed. He liked working in the office. It was warm and much more comfortable than the cab of a delivery van. There was a plentiful supply of coffee and he didn't have to worry about keeping to timetables. His favourite receptionist was also on duty and with a bit of luck he might be in for some of her home-made cake. She had a soft spot for him and Brian knew how to turn on the charm.

Things were quiet in the office and that was exactly how he liked it. He was feeling rather pleased with himself.

What a fright he must have given poor old Georges Pascal when he'd woken him up in the middle of the night. The idea had come to Brian in a flash. It was no good trying to speak to Marian with the woman he took to be her sister hanging around and getting in the way, but her fiancé was a different kettle of fish. He was loaded with money. All these music people were. He'd read the press. They pleaded poverty but he bet they earned more in an evening than a humble delivery driver did in a whole year.

Brian didn't know any Eastern Europeans personally, but he could guess that Georges would be hot-headed. If he suspected his relationship with Marian wasn't on the level, he could start asking awkward questions. Marian wouldn't want to lose her rich boyfriend, so she'd probably go for the easy option and feel more inclined to meet Brian's request for help with paying his living expenses. If not, he was sure he could persuade Georges to cough up. He wouldn't want details of his fiancée's private life plastered all over the press. It would reflect badly on him.

Brian stretched out his long legs under the desk. He had done his homework carefully. He knew exactly where Georges would be staying in Salzburg. It was always at the same hotel. It had been child's play to be put through to his room.

Having stirred things up to his satisfaction, Brian decided it was time to withdraw from the scene and await developments.

'Brought you some walnut cake.' Sara's voice disturbed his thoughts.

'The very thing.' Brian used his smile on her to full effect. A slow blush coloured her cheeks. 'Why don't you sit down next to me? We can enjoy it together,' he suggested.

'I shouldn't really leave the desk unattended,' she said, pretending reluctance, but without much conviction.

'A few minutes won't matter. Besides,

I can see the desk from here. If anyone calls in you can nip back in an instant.' He patted the seat next to his.

'All right,' she agreed.

'This is delicious,' he said, biting off a chunk of walnut fudge icing. 'Did you make it yourself?'

'I like baking cakes,' Sara said, nibbling daintily on a walnut.

'The way to a man's heart,' Brian replied. 'Don't move.' He put out a hand to detain her as one of the drivers' lights flashed on the console. Brian dealt with the query, then turned his attention back to Sara. 'What does a girl like you do of a weekend?'

'I help my mother in the house,' she explained, 'then I walk the dog. I like baking and needlework.'

It was all Brian could do not to grimace. They were hardly the pursuits he looked for in a female. He liked his girlfriends to be lively and to have an edgy past. He also liked to befriend people who could be useful to him. Sara hardly fell into any of these categories, apart from when he was at a loose end in the office, and hungry.

'Any more cake?' he asked as he finished his slice.

'I was keeping some back for the boss,' Sara explained.

'He's out, isn't he?' Brian raised an eyebrow. 'And I won't tell him if you don't.'

Sara bustled away in search of extra supplies of cake. Brian whistled to himself. Life was looking good. He fully expected Marian or Georges to divvy up, then it would be goodbye to this pathetic little job and hello to the sunny spots of the Mediterranean. Brian saw himself with a villa on the French Riviera, or maybe occupying a suite at one of the top hotels. He could even buy a yacht. He'd need a fair bit of money to keep up the lifestyle, but then Marian must have put away a tidy sum over the years. Peter wouldn't be able to help her spend it, so being his brother was the next best thing. It was what Peter would have wanted, Brian thought in an effort to justify his actions. To Peter he was a hero, and that made him feel good. Yes, Peter would have wanted him to have his birth mother's money.

'Here we are.' Sara was back.

'Good grief,' thought Brian, she's actually brought some ditzy paper serviettes decorated with silver hearts.

'These were left over from my sister's wedding reception,' she explained.

'Is that so?' Brian pretended an interest he was far from feeling. Sara needn't think she was going to reel him in. If and when he decided to take the plunge, it wasn't going to be with a girl who worked the reception desk for a delivery firm.

'It was a lovely day.' Sara warmed to her theme. 'Do you like weddings?' she asked innocently.

'As long as they're not my own,' Brian replied. Like a cat playing with a mouse, he enjoyed watching her discomfort.

'I didn't mean that.' She dropped her

cake in her confusion.

Brian looked down at the blouse she was wearing. It looked a bit tight to him, probably from overdoing the cake-eating. He began to grow bored with her company. 'Best get on, I suppose,' he said in a dismissive tone of voice.

'You haven't finished your cake,' Sara sounded disappointed.

'I'm a bit full. I'll leave the rest until later. Isn't that a call coming through on the main switchboard?'

Sara leapt to her feet. 'I hope it's not that funny woman again. She was asking some strange questions.'

'What funny woman?' Brian asked, his instinct now on full alert.

'I'd better answer it.'

Brian's fingers imprisoned Sara's wrist to the table. She winced. 'You're hurting me,' she grimaced.

'What funny woman?' he repeated.

'I don't know. She came in about half an hour ago. Didn't you see her?' Brian shook his head. 'She called up first and said she saw one of our vans in Suffolk parked up during a snowstorm or something.' Sara frowned. 'Isn't that where you were?'

'What else did she say?' Brian demanded.

'Nothing really.' Sara's wide brown eyes were now full of trepidation. 'She wondered if we did removal work in that area. She's clearing out her parents' cottage and thought we might be able to help.'

Brian shot to his feet. 'Did she give you her name?'

'No. I explained we didn't do that type of work but if she thought our company could be of help then we would be more than pleased to provide a quote. I gave her your name as duty controller and a list of our rates and a couple of leaflets. What is it, Brian? What's wrong?'

'Go and answer the call and if it is the same woman tell her to stop pestering us.'

Sara scuttled off, leaving a trail of

cake crumbs on the carpet. Brian snapped his pencil in half, scarcely realising what he was doing. It seemed he had seriously underestimated Marian Barr. He thought that she would be the sort of person who would want to keep her past quiet at any cost. He hadn't figured she'd come looking for him on his own territory. It had been a stupid thing to do to leave his delivery vehicle in full view. Marian must have spotted it. Either that, or her nosy sister had started poking her oar in. Heaven save him from all women.

He paced the office. Now what was he going to do? He couldn't take more unofficial time off. The boss wouldn't swallow another excuse. Brian wasn't in control of the situation, and that was something else he didn't like.

His mobile buzzed in the pocket of his coat.

'Brian?' He recognised his mother's voice, the last person he wanted to speak to right now.

'I'm not supposed to take calls at

work,' he snapped.

'I didn't realise you were at work. I can call back later if it's more convenient.'

'Never mind. Is something wrong?' he asked, hoping he wasn't in for another lecture on how long it was since she had seen him.

'Not really. Only, well . . . you know, I had a guest stay overnight.'

'I told you not to accept bookings for the winter.'

'I know you did, dear.' Peggy Bartholomew sounded confused. 'Only I think I might have done something silly.'

Brian raised his eyes to the ceiling. At times his mother was the stupidest woman in the world. As soon as he got his hands on her money, he was off.

'What sort of silly?' he asked in a patient voice.

'I told her about Peter.'

Brian sagged against his chair in relief. 'I shouldn't let it worry you.'

'It's not only that,' Peggy went on.

'Go on.' Brian tensed up again.

'It was after she'd gone that I realised I might have been indiscreet.'

'In what way?'

'I gave her a photograph of Peter too.'

'Mother,' Brian said, biting down his frustration, 'I really don't have time for all this now. We'll talk next time I come down. I'll try to make it at the weekend. You can do one of your special roast dinners and we'll catch up on all the news then. How does that sound?'

'The thing is,' Peggy continued, 'she said she was his mother.'

11

Marian drew back the curtains and slid open one of the glass doors leading to the patio of her pied-à-terre. The action let in an icy blast of fresh air. She took a deep breath. She loved looking over the River Thames. Its sense of history never failed to interest her and even on the coldest days she would sit out on the balcony in one of her wicker chairs and watch the activity on the water. There was always something going on: tourist boats, water taxis, even filming. She couldn't understand why some of her neighbours preferred to enjoy the air-conditioned sterility of their luxury apartments, hardly bothering to look out of the plate glass windows showcasing one of the most beautiful and famous scenes in the world. Not that Marian knew many of her neighbours. Like her, they were professional people with active lifestyles and rarely at home.

She took another deep breath of bracing air. The winter sun cast a low shadow across the water. It would soon sink behind the buildings opposite. Already the light was fading from the day. She lingered for a few more moments on the small terrace, reluctant to surrender this small island of peace. In her busy life it was rare to have free time, and she wanted to make the most of it.

She had planted two miniature fruit trees in tubs either side of the picture windows. Despite the cold weather, she was pleased to see one was already showing signs of early spring life. The small array of plants she had purchased when she had moved in was a mixture of several varieties. Out of necessity she had also chosen some small ferns that did not require much attention, and an exotic cactus that she had been assured would withstand the harshest weather conditions. She hummed a few notes of one of the pieces she was working on for the charity gala as she watered the fern and tended to the miniature fruit trees.

The programme hadn't been finalised and she realised with a guilty twinge of conscience that neither she nor Georges had given it much attention of late. With so much happening, it had slipped her memory, and when his mind was on other things Georges, too, needed constant reminders about committee meetings and charity obligations.

Reluctantly, Marian abandoned her greenery and went back indoors. The deep velvet curtains made a swishing noise as they closed automatically behind her. She flicked the switch and the room was immediately bathed in subdued peach lighting. Every modern convenience had been catered for, and the décor executed by a highly talented interior designer, but to Marian the apartment never felt like a real home. It boasted every luxury, from a dedicated concierge service to an in-house swimming pool and gymnasium; but despite these benefits, it was only somewhere Marian visited occasionally between concerts and commitments. It was central and convenient, but it had no atmosphere. There were no untidy piles of magazines, or discarded coffee mugs, or dog hairs on the furniture. Everything looked as though it had recently been unwrapped.

Georges had mentioned living in London after they were married. He occupied a suite in a hotel when he was in the city, but Marian's preference was for somewhere by the sea. She didn't like air conditioning. She needed to breathe real air, to smell the sea and to feel the wind in her hair and to hear the waves lapping the shore.

She smiled as she read again the text Georges had sent her after he had arrived back in Salzburg. Richard's rage had subsided now his star performer had returned to work. He had even managed to grab some publicity out of the incident, citing Georges' love for his beautiful fiancée. Marian had grimaced over that one as the reason for his absence. The promoters had been assured such a thing wouldn't happen again. The popular press had looked on his antics with an indulgent eye, but Marian imagined Georges would have to exercise the full extent of his charm to wriggle out of the trouble he was in. Fortunately, he lived in a world of temperaments and she hoped he would be forgiven this one small transgression. It gave Marian a small thrill to realise he had been willing to sacrifice his career, impulsive and misguided though the action was, because he thought she had a lover.

She speed-dialled Sally's number but again was diverted to voice mail. Marian bit down her irritation, then tried Sally's home number. Again there was no reply. Hoping Ian or one of the children might pick up her calls, Marian left a message.

That only left the chair of the charity committee. Marian unearthed her paperwork and dialled the number.

'I realise the snow was responsible, Miss Barr,' Mrs Mitchell said after Marian apologised for not having been in touch. 'Half the committee's travel plans were disrupted so the agenda was put on hold. Perhaps we can reschedule when Mr Pascal is back in the country? I can't tell you how popular he is.' She gave a girlish laugh. 'I've been reading about his antics in my newspaper. I wish my husband would do that sort of thing.'

Marian blushed as she remembered how ardent Georges' lovemaking had been afterwards. Finally free of her past, her own responses had been equally as uninhibited.

'Enquiries about the concert and requests for advance tickets are extremely healthy.' Mrs Mitchell's voice drew Marian back to the present. 'We confidently predict we will have a success on our hands.'

'That's excellent news. By the way,

my sister said she might make apologies on my behalf. I don't suppose you heard from her?' Marian enquired.

'I haven't, no,' Mrs Mitchell replied.

Marian sat down in front of her baby grand. She needed to practise. Her fingers would stiffen up if she didn't. They also began to itch if a day passed without any musical activity, and she had not had access to an instrument for nearly a week. She chose a few simple warm-up exercises and scales to loosen her fingers and to get her into practice mode. As a soloist she was responsible for stamping her finger-print on every performance. Every artist possessed individual dynamics and it was up to them to ignite audience response. It was his or her interpretation of a particular piece that would ensure their popularity when it came to ticket sales and advance bookings. In a world where supply excelled demand, Marian knew it was vital not to let standards slip.

There was always an army of talented young wannabees in the wings, fresh out of the conservatoires and more than willing to step into her shoes.

Marian's love of the piano swept aside all other considerations and when she was practising she would forget everything else — the time, meals, appointments. Music was the one constant in her life, and until she had met Georges, her only love. It had seen her through some bad days and had never let her down, even during her darkest hours.

She was breathing heavily by the time she finished her last étude. A glance at the clock informed her she had been playing for over two hours. She closed the piano lid, stood up and stretched her aching limbs. She was tired, but happily tired. Crossing to her bag, she retrieved the photo of Peter that Mrs Bartholomew had given to her. He was wearing school uniform. His shirt collar was askew, his tie undone, and he was scowling at the camera in the same way his father used to scowl if something displeased him. The resemblance was striking. A lump clogged Marian's throat. Although she knew she had no right to call herself Peter's mother, she couldn't help feeling a mother's pride and anguish over the loss of the son she never knew.

Going to her music case, she retrieved the yellow plastic duck from where she had hidden it. They were all that she had left of Peter. Whoever had sent the threatening letter and made the menacing telephone call to Hatpin Cottage no longer had the power to hurt her. He had made a mistake contacting Georges. That had been the catalyst for her confession.

Georges was a man with intense physical needs; and now there were no longer secrets in her past to haunt her, Marian too was free to express her love. She shivered. There had been no other men in her life, apart from Valentin, and her very brief relationship with Ian before Sally had decided he was the man for her.

Her heartbeat quickened. Until now she had felt inhibited in her love life with Georges, but with all barriers finally removed there was no reason for her to hold back any longer, especially not in a city like Paris.

Marian inspected the contents of her wardrobe. It was at times like this when she wished she had help, but Marian had always declined the services of a personal assistant. The thought of someone knowing the intimate details of her life had always discouraged her. She suspected it stemmed from years of glossing over her past. She closed the door with a soft thud and opened the drawers of her cupboard. A quick search confirmed that some of the more intimate items of her wardrobe were in desperate need of an update. Tomorrow morning she had to go shopping for some lingerie.

The ringing of the telephone drew her back into the drawing room.

'Sally?' Her sister's mobile number flashed up on the display. 'I've left messages for you all over the place. Where on earth have you been?'

The line went dead.

12

Georges had shown Marian a Paris she never knew existed. Together they had explored tiny back streets, seeking out local delicacies, then enjoyed al fresco picnics of cheeses, patés, bread and wine in secluded parks as they watched the world go by.

'Everyone does the boulevard bit.' Georges smiled at Marian's reaction when she had gasped in delight at the charming landscaped garden she would never have expected to find in the middle of such a bustling city as Paris. It was tucked away behind a pretty church in a leafy corner of a cobbled square.

'But I don't want to sit in a pavement café while we watch the world go by. I am selfish. I don't want to have to share you with anyone else.'

His voice was a low murmur against

her ear and his words brought a blush to her cheeks. Marian, too, didn't feel like being sociable. Normally she enjoyed winding down with like-minded friends where the talk would be of music and the performing arts, but not this visit. Together they had taken off away from the hubbub a tour always created. Both their agents had been outraged at their lack of regard for the media, but neither Georges nor Marian minded.

'You need to be seen,' Richard protested. 'You have to put yourself about.'

'When I am working I give one hundred and ten percent of myself. When I am not, I don't. It is as simple as that,' Georges explained.

★　★　★

'We should think about a date for our wedding.' Georges leaned back against a convenient tree stump and sipped his red wine. He narrowed his blue eyes.

The afternoon sun was so brilliant it almost turned them green. 'Or do you have any more surprises to pull out of the hat for me?'

'You know I don't.' Marian sliced into a succulent peach and passed a segment over to Georges.

Although it was the wrong season for the summer fruit, they had discovered a market street stall bursting with produce of every description. Together they had been unable to resist the plump choices on display under the green and white striped awning; and although Marian suspected the stallholder, with a shrewd eye to a purchase, had inflated the prices, they had chosen two peaches and some plump black cherries also out of season but which the stallholder had assured them were the sweetest in Europe.

'I have to go to America,' Georges said. 'The trip was planned over a year ago. I need to talk to the promoters of a proposed West Coast tour.' He shrugged. 'I will try to get back as soon as I can, but these things have to be done. Richard will be with me. He strikes a hard bargain but he needs my presence to seal the deal.'

Marian nibbled on her peach and did her best to quell her racing heartbeat. The idea of a second marriage still made her nervous, but she was convinced she was doing the right thing — although it would mean huge adjustments to both their personal lives.

'You don't want a big ceremony, do you?' Georges' fingertips brushed hers as he took another piece of fruit. 'I have few family. You have Sally, of course, but otherwise I have no one I would like to invite. We could have a small civil ceremony followed by a blessing? Or maybe a party in the summer?'

'Whatever you say,' Marian agreed with a lazy sigh, wondering when she would see her sister again.

Their only contact had been the aborted telephone call when the connection had been cut. Tired of leaving messages that were never returned,

160

Marian decided to get on with her own life. No doubt in time Sally would be in touch.

Marian hadn't thought she would ever be so happy. Georges still proved to be a gentle and considerate lover and she knew at last she could put her past demons to rest.

'What would you like to do this evening?' Georges asked as they began to pack up their things. 'I would have suggested dinner on a *bateau mouche* but I think it will be too cold to go on the river.' He shivered. 'I know I come from a harsh climate but I do not like the winter. Maybe we could go somewhere warm like Italy for our honeymoon? Although,' his voice was almost a purr, 'you do not need the sun to look more beautiful than you do now.'

A young family strolled by and they exchanged greetings. Marian no longer felt the familiar stab of pain the sight of children used to cause her. When the little boy had smiled up at her she had returned his friendly wave, and with their mother's permission offered him and his sister some of their cherries. The children had fallen on them in delight and Marian had listened to their excited chatter as they'd skipped away, an indulgent smile on her lips.

'Am I supposed to say you look beautiful too?' she teased him.

'It would be nice,' Georges admitted, his familiar smile tugging the corners of his mouth. 'I'm very vain, you know. When you are a maestro it goes with the territory.'

'In that case,' Marian responded firmly, 'maestro or not, you have no need for me to tell you how wonderful you are. There are enough women in your life more than willing to heap praise on you.'

'Alas, that is true,' Georges replied with false modesty, 'but I don't happen to be in love with any of them.' He leaned forward and kissed Marian gently on the lips. 'You taste of cherries,' he said, running his hands through her hair, 'and red wine, an exotic combination that is tripling my pulse.'

'Georges, everyone can see.' Marian wriggled uncomfortably on the grass as his kisses grew more urgent.

'I don't care, if you don't.' Georges was unfazed by her reprimand. 'You need to shake off your past inhibitions and I intend to show you how.'

'All the same, it's only half past three in the afternoon and we are in a public place, overlooked by windows. I'm sure I saw a net curtain twitch.' She did her best not to succumb to Georges' charm. 'I don't know about you but I don't want to spend the night in police custody.'

'Then let us go back to our hotel room.'

'Don't you want to do more sightseeing?' she asked.

'No,' Georges replied, 'and sitting on cold grass is not much fun. It would be much warmer indoors. I will enjoy peeling off some of that delicious new lingerie you have purchased.' He drew her gently to her feet. The feel of his body against hers broke down the last of Marian's resistance.

'I like to see you smile,' Georges said. 'In the past your eyes have been too sad. Now they are alight with life.' He entwined his fingers through hers. 'Shall we walk back?'

She shivered, not entirely from the cold. 'Let's take a taxi,' she suggested.

'Another very good idea,' Georges agreed with her, and as if by magic a cab drew up beside them. Jumping in, Georges gave the driver the name of their hotel before sinking into the back seat. The cab smelt of stale tobacco, although there was a notice asking the patrons not to smoke. Marian wound down the window a fraction.

'You British and your love of fresh air,' he chided her.

'It's good for you.'

'So are spring greens, but I don't like them.'

Marian laughed for no other reason

than she felt happy. The driver looked in his rear view mirror with the tolerant smile that French men of his age seemed to reserve for lovers. Marian blushed. Was it so obvious?

Slow rain began to mist the windscreen and soon the cobble-stoned sidewalks were glistening wet. Pedestrians huddled under umbrellas as the pavement artists hurriedly covered up their work.

'You are English?' the driver asked.

'I am,' Marian replied. 'My fiancé is half French.'

'Then for you, mademoiselle, I have ordered your weather to make you feel at home.'

'Thank you.'

'De rien,' he replied, and winked at her.

Georges stirred beside her, a frown drawing his eyebrows together. 'Stop encouraging his attention,' he ground out through tightened lips.

'Nearly there,' Marian said in an attempt to lighten his mood as the cab crossed the Seine in the direction of St Germain des Prés towards their hotel. They had chosen to stay in a quiet corner of a bustling tourist area in a small 17th century converted town-house hotel that boasted a tiny inner courtyard garden. The owner was an old friend of Georges; he had stayed there many times and knew his privacy would not be invaded by fans eager to get a piece of the famous Georges Pascal.

'Even Richard doesn't know our whereabouts,' he had confided to Marian, 'and I know I can trust Emil not to divulge them.'

Emil was waiting for them on the doorstep as they drew up outside.

'There was no need to welcome us back,' Georges greeted him after he paid off the driver.

'There was a telephone call for you, Georges,' Emil explained with a look of apology.

'Who from?'

'Mr Walton. I don't know how your

agent discovered your whereabouts. All the members of my staff are very discreet. I am sure none of them would have divulged details of your presence in the hotel.'

'I'm sure they didn't,' Georges reassured Emil, 'and I'm not blaming you.'

'What does Richard want now?' Marian demanded.

'I don't know. I deliberately kept my diary empty.'

'He said it was something to do with America? I tried to tell him you were not here but he did not believe me.'

'Perhaps you had better call him back,' Marian advised. 'I'm sure Richard wouldn't have tried to contact you unless it was absolutely necessary.'

'Do you know where he is?' Georges asked Emil.

'He gave me this number.'

Georges glanced at it. 'His London office,' he said.

'You are welcome to use the hotel telephone,' Emil offered after Georges explained he had deliberately left his mobile phone behind in Salzburg. 'Perhaps I could also offer you a glass of house red with my compliments while you are thinking what to do?'

'We'll be in the courtyard,' Georges replied.

Marian stifled her disappointment. In her opinion, Richard abused Georges' professionalism. She didn't know how he had found out their number but he would have known Georges would be unable to ignore his call.

'I don't like being parted from you at this time, especially as you may still have a stalker,' he said.

'I can deal with him,' Marian replied, having almost forgotten about the disturbing telephone call and the anonymous letter.

Emil appeared with a tray of drinks and put them down on the table.

'Would you dial the number for me?' Georges asked him.

'With pleasure.'

Marian trawled through her messages

while Georges attended to his call. Unlike him, she had brought her mobile along with her, although she hadn't glanced at it since their arrival. Sally's home number flashed up several times.

She glanced towards the reception desk to where Georges was now in animated conversation with Richard. She could tell by his gestures the exchange was growing heated.

Swiftly she dialled Sally's number. Her husband Ian immediately answered the call.

'You're back,' she greeted her brother-in-law. 'Was it a good trip?'

'No different from any other business trip,' he replied briskly. 'Where are you?'

'Paris,' she replied.

'Is Sally with you?'

'I thought she might be with you.'

'I haven't seen her since she took off for Suffolk to your parents' cottage. Did you see her there?'

'Yes, but I was called away. When I

got back Sally had already left.'

'Then where is she? She isn't answering her calls and she hasn't been in contact with any of her friends.'

'Have you tried the children?'

'I don't want to worry them. Did she have anything on her mind, do you know?' Ian asked.

'Er,' Marian hesitated, wondering if he knew about David Hicks.

'You might as well know we had a robust difference of opinion before she left. It's nothing new. You know what Sally's like. Sometimes I think she thrives on confrontation. I leave her to have a good sulk, then life usually returns to normal. I thought she would be here when I got back.'

'And she isn't?'

'Marian,' Ian sounded distraught, 'I think she's disappeared.'

13

Marian had plenty of time to think things over on the Eurostar. As the train thundered through the tunnel, then out into the winter sunshine of the Kent countryside, she tried to get her thoughts in order. Not wanting to alarm Ian or to tell tales on her sister, she had done her best to reassure him that she was sure Sally was fine and had probably only gone off on one of her jaunts.

'You know Sally,' she had said, injecting a light note into her voice. 'Always searching for thrills.'

Ian had not been convinced. 'She doesn't normally disappear for days on end without contacting anyone or at least telling someone where she is going. You last saw her in Suffolk at Hatpin Cottage?'

'Yes,' Marian replied guardedly, hoping

Ian wasn't going to start asking searching questions. Her thoughts turned to the jacket found on the beach and the subsequent telephone call from the police. Marian was beginning to wonder if David Hicks had anything to do with Sally's mysterious disappearance. Had they eventually met up? Had they clicked, and had he persuaded her to go off with him? It didn't seem plausible, but Marian wasn't sure about anything anymore; and with Sally, you never knew what she would get up to.

'Then as far as I can make out that's the last time anyone saw her,' Ian said. 'She wasn't at the cottage when you got back from your business trip?'

'No.' Marian shifted position uncomfortably in her seat. Privately she shared Ian's fears. Things were not looking good.

As she had been speaking to Ian on the telephone, a noise from the reception desk distracted Marian and she glanced across to where Georges was finishing his call to Richard Walton.

172

'I blame myself,' Ian was saying. 'I should never have said half the things I did, but it was almost as if Sally wanted to have an argument. Lately I don't know what's got into her. Did you notice anything odd in her behaviour?'

'Ian, I have to go.'

'What? Oh, right. Fine. Can you call me when you're back from Paris? I don't want to contact the authorities but I may have to.'

Doing her best to persuade her brother-in-law to wait a day or so before taking any further action, Marian turned to Georges, who was now by her side.

'Richard would like me to fly to New York in the morning,' he said.

'How did he find out where we were?' Marian demanded with a frown, realising that if Richard could track them down then so too could Brian or David Hicks.

'Mrs Wren. I've just been in touch with her. She admits Richard bullied her into giving out our whereabouts.

She apologises for disrupting our mini break.' Georges raised his shoulders in a gesture of amused tolerance. 'We all know how persuasive Richard can be when he is after something, and although it is out of character Mrs Wren fell victim to his technique. What else can I say?'

'Not to worry.' Marian did her best to keep her smile neutral. She didn't want Georges to suspect that after what Ian had told her she had butterflies dancing a tango in her stomach.

'It will mean dining in and an early night if I am to be off first thing in the morning. Emil has a good chef and he has promised us something special.'

Their last night in Paris was as magical as their first. Glowing in the happiness of her new-found love, Marian had not fallen asleep until the winter sun began to cast cinnamon strips of light across the Paris rooftops. Emil had tapped discreetly on the bedroom door with a tray of coffee, fresh croissants and a bowl of apricots while Georges showered, ready for an early start.

Within half an hour the taxi had called to take him to Charles de Gaulle airport and, assuring her this was absolutely the last time Richard would disrupt their plans, Georges had jumped into the cab. Mrs Wren, eager to make up for her indiscretion, had arranged for someone to meet him in New York with a change of clothes and everything he would need for his onward journey to the West Coast.

Marian had partaken of her breakfast at a more leisurely pace, before heading for the Gare du Nord to catch the train back to St Pancras. She didn't know any of Sally's friends so was unable to check if she had been visiting them; and anyway, she presumed Ian would have checked before calling her. Without holding out much hope, Marian dialled Sally's number, but the line was dead. There was no redirection of messages to voice mail. Marian's twinge of panic deepened.

Where could she have gone? What had she done? Marian's head ached from the pressure.

All too soon the train drew into St Pancras, and Marian was no nearer to finding an answer. Calling Ian from the taxi, he confirmed that he too had heard nothing from her.

'What do you suggest we do?' Marian asked, wishing Georges were here by her side, hot-headed though he could be on occasions. Now they had no secrets from each other, she missed his presence. He was the one person she could rely on in a crisis.

'Perhaps we should retrace her footsteps?'

'You mean go back to the cottage?'

'That was the last place you saw Sally, wasn't it?'

Marian bit her lip. Although it wasn't her secret, she had to tell Ian about David Hicks.

'I believe she had made an appointment to meet someone there,' she began.

'Who?' Ian demanded.

'An old friend, but he didn't turn up.'

'Who is this old friend?' Ian asked.

'He was part of the crowd Sally used to go around with before she met you.'

'I see.' Ian's reply was full of meaning. 'So he's an old boyfriend?'

'I don't think things were serious between them,' Marian hastened to add.

'I know it's an awful lot to ask of you, Marian,' — to her relief Ian dropped the subject of old boyfriends — 'but do you have the time to go back up to Hatpin Cottage?'

'I was scheduled to be in Paris, but Georges was called away to America; so yes, I have the time. The cottage still needs to be cleared out.'

'In that case, can I meet you up there later this evening? I've one or two things to do before I can leave.'

The snow had completely thawed now, and after a hurried trip to her London apartment Marian retrieved her car from the underground parking area and completed the drive in good time. Without the backdrop of a lowering sky full of threatening clouds, the cottage looked less stark, and she noticed with pleasure small buds pushing through the damp tufts of grass by the gate. The air smelt green and fresh. It was impossible to imagine anything nasty happening here. It was easier to convince herself that there had to be a logical explanation for Sally's disappearance.

Marian unlocked the heavy wooden front door and pushed it open. It was obvious Sally hadn't been back. Her sister's dropped box of pencils was exactly where Marian had placed it on the coffee table.

Ian wouldn't be arriving for a few more hours but Marian was reluctant to get involved in anything too heavy, in case she had to abandon her plans at short notice. Pulling back the curtains, she looked out of the window at the back garden. It wasn't very big, with its small patch of grass and the circular rose bed her mother had planted in the middle of the lawn. Marian saw to her regret that with no one to tend it, the flowerbed was becoming overgrown.

The ghost of a smile hovered on Marian's lips. The family had suffered its fair share of mishaps over the years, but what family didn't? Marian had always felt safe here, and she was sure it was the same with Sally. Their parents' love had been the one constant in their lives. She had to keep positive, Marian told herself as she inspected the various items Sally had been sorting through before she took off.

There was no evidence of a break-in, so Sally must have left of her own free will. Marian glanced at the telephone. Her parents were uncomfortable with technology. They did not believe in answering machines and didn't see the need to have one, so there was no way Marian could check if any calls had been received. Without much hope, she dialled one-four-seven-one to check on the last recorded call. The number was not one she recognised and had been received when Marian had been visiting Peggy Bartholomew. Sally must have spoken to someone.

Scribbling down the number on a notepad, Marian put a hand to her chest to steady her swiftly beating heart before she plucked up the courage to dial the number. She was working out what to say when a man answered.

'I'm sorry, who did you say you were?' she began.

'Who is this?' he demanded in an unfriendly tone of voice.

'You dialled this number a few days ago and I'm returning your call.'

'You still haven't answered my question.'

'My name is Marian Barr and I'm in Suffolk.'

'You aren't by any chance related to a woman called Sally something-or-other?'

'Yes, I am.' Marian did her best to keep her excitement out of her voice. 'Do you know where my sister is?'

'I have absolutely no idea, but she left

a strange message on my answer phone saying she had tracked me down to Essex, then she gave a silly laugh and apologised because she realised she had called the wrong number. It may have been funny to her but it frightened the life out of my wife when she played it back. Then my wife began to suspect I was having an affair. When I called your sister to give her a piece of mind, there was no reply.'

'I'm so sorry,' Marian began.

'Suffolk, you say? Then let me tell you, if I get any more calls from you or members of your cerebrally challenged family, I won't hesitate to track you down to this Suffolk place of yours. Do I make myself clear? Now leave us alone. You've caused enough trouble.'

Marian winced as the receiver was crashed down in her ear. The phone sprang into life as soon as she hung up.

'Hello?' she asked cautiously as she picked it up.

'Miss Barr?' a female voice enquired.

'Yes,' Marian replied carefully, hoping

she wasn't in for another tirade of abuse.

'I'm so glad you're in. I wasn't sure what to do. I wanted to contact you earlier, but then I thought you would probably feel it was an invasion of your privacy or something like that, and . . . well, um, I wanted to talk to you.'

'My agent deals with any publicity material you may be requesting,' Marian replied. She always did her best to be polite to fans, but sometimes she was staggered by the extent of their ingenuity. How this one had managed to track down her parents' private telephone number was beyond her.

'I don't understand.' The caller now sounded even more uncertain. 'I got this number from the visitors' book you signed. It's Peggy Bartholomew here.'

Marian didn't realise she had been holding her breath until a pain in her chest forced her to expel a sigh of relief.

'Peggy, hello.'

A wall of silence met her reply.

'Is there anything I can do for you?' Marian asked.

'No, not really.'

'May I know why you're calling me?' Sensing undertones, Marian kept her voice deliberately gentle.

'It's Brian,' Peggy admitted.

'Your son?' Marian's knuckles whitened as she gripped the receiver.

'I'm worried about him — or rather, what he might do.'

'I don't understand,' Marian replied.

'I told you he was a delivery driver.'

'Yes.'

'For a firm in Essex.'

Marian stiffened. Essex again. It couldn't be a coincidence. Sally must have been trying to track him down.

'I — ' Peggy cleared her throat. 'He travels so much, I wasn't too sure where he was, because it's been a while since I've seen him. I called his mobile number. I was only going to leave a voice mail message. They are such useful things, aren't they? Mobile telephones?'

'Yes,' Marian replied, wishing Peggy would get to the point.

'Sorry, I'm not putting this very well,

am I? I spoke to Brian. He said he had been asked to cover in the office during his boss's absence. Actually, he sounded a bit annoyed. He doesn't like personal calls when he's working. Anyway, I told him about you.'

'What?' Marian snapped.

'I told him about your visit and that I'd given you Peter's photo.'

'Why?'

'It was foolish of me, I know, but I thought if he found out later what I'd done and that I hadn't told him, he might not be very pleased. I'm sorry.'

'Peggy, you mustn't be scared of your son,' Marian chided her.

'I'm not, really. I mean, I know he was jealous of Peter, but that was my fault.'

'Why was it your fault?'

'I suppose I spoilt Peter. He was the youngest. You know, the much-longed-for second child.'

Peggy's voice faltered. Marian sensed she knew what was coming.

'Did you tell Brian I am Peter's birth

mother?' she prompted.

'Yes I did. That's why I'm calling you. I wouldn't want to cause you any more trouble, and sometimes . . . well, Brian tends to see things in black and white. There's no in-between with him. He might feel . . . ' Her voice faded. 'I'm not sure what exactly, but I thought it best to warn you. He has a temper, you see, like his father. He may come looking for you.' She finished on an uncertain note.

'To do what?'

'I don't know. His jealousy of Peter was very intense.'

'Mrs Bartholomew — Peggy — ' Marian hastened to reassure her. 'There's no need to worry. My fiancé knows all about Peter and my first marriage. There's nothing Brian can do to damage my reputation.'

'That is a relief, but there's something else you ought to know — something I ought to have told you before now.'

'What's that?'

'It was an accident, of course, and there was nothing to suggest otherwise.'

Another cold chill of fear worked its way up Marian's spine.

'Brian was totally cracked up after it happened. You see, he was driving the car the day of the accident. Peter was his passenger. He'd been to collect him from swimming practice. He swerved to avoid an oncoming vehicle. It is a notorious stretch of road. People drive far too fast along it. No way was Brian at fault, but he lost control of the car. His father and I never blamed him, but I think he blamed himself. He saw a psychiatrist for a short while after it happened.' Peggy's voice trailed off. 'But I don't think she did any good. Brian was still as disturbed as ever. Are you still there?' she asked.

'Yes, I'm still here,' Marian managed to reply through a sea of pain and sickness.

'I thought you ought to know.'

There was a gentle click as the receiver was replaced.

14

'Can I help you, sir?' The sergeant looked up as a dishevelled member of the public approached his desk. To the police officer's trained eye, he looked as though he had been sleeping rough.

'I'm not sure.' The man gave a shaky smile.

'Are you all right? Why don't you sit down while I'll get you a cup of tea?' he offered with a concerned look.

'Thank you,' he replied, 'that would be very nice.'

'Won't be a moment, sir. Make yourself comfortable.'

He was back within minutes, carrying a tray of tea.

'There you are, sir. It's hot, sweet and strong, just the thing for shock.'

'I need to talk to someone.'

'Why don't you come into one of the interview rooms? That way we'll get some privacy. Give me a moment and I'll arrange reception cover.' The policeman opened a door to a side office. 'Go in, sir. Don't forget your tea.'

The man sat down at the plain wooden desk and sipped his drink. Slowly some colour returned to his face. He unzipped his wax jacket and, taking it off, draped it around the back of his seat. The door opened and he looked up.

'All sorted. Now,' the sergeant said, drawing up a chair and sitting down. 'What can I do for you?'

'I'm not sure you can do anything. It's a bit complicated.'

'Why don't you give me your name, for starters? You don't mind if I take notes?'

'My name is David Hicks.'

'Right, Mr Hicks. What seems to be the problem?'

'I would have come to see you earlier, only I had a bit of an accident and I temporarily lost my memory.'

'I see.' The sergeant began scribbling on his pad of paper. 'Has your memory now returned?'

'Bits of it, although there are gaps,' David admitted.

'Have you seen a doctor?'

'No, but I don't want to, not yet anyway.'

'I can arrange a check up for you, sir.'

'Later perhaps.'

'As you wish. Are you up to telling me why you are here?'

'I read in the newspaper about the abandoned jacket that was found on the beach.'

'Was it yours?' The sergeant began to take more of an interest in the man sitting opposite him.

'I think it might have been. Mine was old a tweed one I got from a charity shop.'

'That does fit the description of the jacket we found. You can look at it later. There was a telephone number in the pocket . . . ' The police officer looked expectantly at David.

'I think there might have been,' he admitted, 'but I'm not sure. Some things are still a bit blurred.'

'Were you due to pay a visit to Miss Barr?' the sergeant prompted him.

'Yes and no.'

'Sorry?'

'I was due to meet Mrs Rogers.'

'Who is Mrs Rogers?'

'Barr was her maiden name. Mr and Mrs Barr were her parents. They used to live at Hatpin Cottage.'

'That was the telephone number on the slip of paper we found in the pocket.'

'Was it? Anyway, Mrs Rogers was visiting the area and we arranged to meet up, but I didn't make it.'

'If we could go back a bit, sir,' the sergeant stopped him. 'All this was over a week ago. Where have you been?'

'That's what I'm trying to tell you. After I banged my head, I wandered around for a bit. I was disorientated and couldn't work out where I was.'

'Why did you take off your jacket and

leave it on the beach? It was an extremely cold day.'

'I needed to wash the blood off my shirt.'

'Had you cut yourself?'

'My head.' David frowned. 'I thought I told you? I fell.'

'Then what happened?' the sergeant asked in a deliberately neutral tone of voice.

'A lady came by. She was walking her dog and he pounced on my jacket and ran off with it. I went to chase after him but I fell over again in the snow. The lady could see I had been injured and she took me back to her caravan to bathe my head. In all the confusion I forgot about the jacket. She lent me this one.' He indicated the wax jacket on the back of his chair.

'Who is this lady?'

'She's a traveller. Her name is Gypsy Jenny. She had lots of herbs and potions and stuff in her caravan and she dressed my wounds. Then she gave me something to drink. It made me feel pretty woozy and I fell asleep.'

'If you'll forgive me for saying so, sir, this all sounds a bit far-fetched.'

'You don't believe my story?'

'Let's put it this way, sir: I do need a few more details.'

'It's true,' David insisted.

'All right. I'll go along with it for the moment. You say you stayed with Gypsy Jenny all this time?'

'She was going to move on — she tells fortunes and sells beads at craft fairs — only the weather delayed her, so we spent our days playing cards, reading, going for walks, things like that. She told me my memory would come back, given time.'

'I see.' The sergeant gave him a sceptical look.

'It does take some believing, doesn't it?' David admitted.

'Indeed it does, sir. Do you want me to contact Mrs Rogers for you, tell her you are all right and explain what happened? She might be worried about you.'

'No.' David's voice went up an octave.

'All right, sir. Calm down.'

'I haven't finished my story. I've hardly started it.'

'The floor's yours, sir.'

'I didn't know anything about any police involvement in my disappearance until we found an old newspaper swept up on the beach when we were out walking Jenny's dog. Did I say she's a bit of a recluse? She doesn't even have a radio in her caravan. When I read about a jacket being handed in to the police, and that you were appealing for the owner to come forward, I realised it might be mine and that I might be in some sort of trouble.'

'And are you?'

'I don't know.'

'When did your memory start to come back?'

'Yesterday morning. I was making tea when Jenny's dog barked to be let back in. It made me jump. There isn't much room in the caravan and I knocked my head on a cupboard. As I rubbed at the bump I began to remember a few things.'

'As I say, that's quite some story, sir.'

'I didn't make it up,' David insisted.

'Nevertheless, there are huge gaps in it, as I'm sure you must realise.'

David blinked at the policeman.

'Where are your family?'

'I don't have any, none that I'm close to anyway.'

'So no one would have missed you in your absence?'

'I doubt it.'

'Surely you had some form of identify on you — credit cards, a driving licence? How did you get to Suffolk? I'm presuming you don't come from this part of the world. Did you drive up here? If so, where is your car? How did you get the telephone number of Hatpin Cottage?'

'I'm coming to that.' David's eyes flickered nervously. 'Could I have some water?'

The sergeant poured him a glass and

passed it across the desk. David took a long swallow. 'Thank you.'

'Do you feel ready to continue now?'

David nodded. 'I don't use credit cards. I don't drive either. I caught a train.'

'From where?'

'Sutton. It's in Surrey. I live in a bed-sit.'

'Right.'

'Where was I?'

'At the station?' the policeman prompted.

'That's right. It was snowing quite heavily when I arrived.'

'What did you do then?'

'I hung around for a bit, then I managed to hitch a lift from a delivery driver. He had stopped to drop off a little old lady. We helped her with her shopping. He was going my way so I jumped in his van, but then the weather closed in and it was impossible to see anything. We came across an old barn, so we took refuge there. It was warm and dry inside and the driver and I got talking. I told him I was making for Hatpin Cottage. When he asked why, I explained I had an appointment to meet someone and that we had something of a personal nature to discuss.'

'Who was this driver?'

'I'm coming to that.'

'Go on then.'

'He asked if I was due to meet a Miss Barr. As you know, before her marriage Sally's name was Barr, so I said yes. By now I was beginning to feel a bit uneasy.'

'Why's that, sir?'

'It was the way he kept asking me questions, and he was giving me some strange looks and behaving a bit oddly.'

'What was this personal business you had to discuss with Mrs Rogers?'

'Sally and I were friends a long time ago. We weren't really close, but we used to go around with the same crowd. It was nothing more than that.' David shot a challenging look at the police officer.

'But you kept in touch with her over the years?'

'No.'

'You didn't keep in touch?'

David shook his head. 'She did rather well for herself after she married. Life wasn't quite so kind to me and we didn't really move in the same circles any more. Our lives drifted in different directions.'

'I understand.'

David looked at the policeman with a puzzled frown as if the effort of remembering what had happened was too much for him.

'Do you remember your driver companion's name?'

'He didn't give it to me. I don't really know how it happened, but for some reason he got a bit heated and started accusing me of trying to get in on his act.'

'His act?'

'He said he was due to meet Miss Barr as well. From what he said, I realised we were talking about two different people and that he must be referring to Sally's sister. She's the concert pianist Marian Barr.'

'I've spoken to the lady.'

'You have?'

'We telephoned her from the station to ask if she knew anything about your coat. She didn't.'

'I didn't know she was going to be at Hatpin Cottage,' David mumbled. 'I wish I'd never heard of the place either.'

'Do you know Miss Barr?'

'Not really. I may have seen her once or twice but Sally's older than her sister and when we used to go around together Marian was away studying music, I think. I'm not really sure.'

'As I understand it, Miss Barr and Mrs Rogers were meeting up at the cottage with a view to going through their parents' things before putting the property on the market. Mr Pascal was there as well.'

'Who is Mr Pascal?' David asked.

'He is Miss Barr's fiancé.'

'It's all beginning to make sense

now.' David's brow cleared.

'Is it?' the sergeant raised his eyebrows.

'Sally lives in Berkshire.'

'Yes?'

'I live in Surrey. It's a bit of a journey for me to get to her, but not nearly as far as coming all the way up here. I couldn't understand why she paid my train fare and insisted I come to Suffolk, but I think Sally wanted to be with her sister and this Mr Pascal when we met up, and that's why she suggested I came up here as well.'

'You mean she didn't want to see you on her own?'

'It looks like that, doesn't it?'

'Why would that be?'

David lapsed into silence.

'If Mrs Rogers didn't want to see you on her own, surely the easiest thing to do would be to see you in her husband's presence?'

'No, you don't understand.' David put out a hand and grabbed at the sergeant's sleeve.

'Then enlighten me.'

'You won't arrest me, will you? I mean, I came here of my own free will.'

The sergeant took a discreet look at his watch. 'Perhaps I ought to consult one of my superior officers.'

'I prefer to talk to you.'

'All right, sir, and we won't be arresting you unless you've done something wrong.'

'It's that delivery driver you should be arresting.'

'We're back to him now, are we, sir?'

'I can't prove anything, and he would probably say I slipped on some ice or something, but I'm sure he's the reason why I banged my head.'

'Why would he attack you?'

'I told you. He seemed jealous of my relationship with Mrs Rogers, or Miss Barr as he called her. Anyway, if I really did slip over, why wasn't he around when I came to my senses?'

'You tell me, sir.'

'He'd driven off after he attacked me, that's why.'

'And you've no idea where he went until you came to?' The sergeant made a note. 'Exactly where was this, sir?'

'I wasn't in the barn place. I was near the beach; that's why I went down to the water to wash off the blood. It's all coming back much more clearly now.'

'I'm pleased to hear that, sir. And this driver — you haven't seen or heard from him since?'

'No.'

'And you don't want to speak to Mrs Rogers?'

'Not really. You see,' David said, sipping more water, 'the reason I made arrangements to see her was because . . . well, I wanted money from her.'

'I guessed as much, sir.'

'You did?'

'I can't think of any other reason why Mrs Rogers would want to meet up with you. Your paths haven't crossed over the years, and then out of the blue — and I'm guessing here — you turn up on her doorstep?'

201

'At first she was pleased to see me, and we went for a coffee and chatted about old times. She gave me some money. I didn't ask for it,' David hastened to add. 'She volunteered it.'

'Then you came back for more?'

'She seemed a soft touch and I sort of played on our past relationship. I feel so ashamed of how I behaved. Living with Jenny over the past week has made me realise there's more to life than material things. If you do see Mrs Rogers — Sally — will you apologise to her, and tell her I'm sorry, and that I won't be causing her any more trouble?'

'You've got a police record, haven't you, sir?'

'How can you tell?'

'Years of experience. I always know. Is that the hold you had over Mrs Rogers? Was that the price of your silence?'

David nodded. 'It happened when we were young. We were all at a party and some other stuff went on at the same time. You don't need the details?'

'Not if it's not relevant, sir.'

'It isn't. Anyway, we both did time. I'm sure Sally's been a law-abiding citizen ever since.'

'But her past indiscretion wasn't something she wanted her family or her neighbours to know about?'

'Would you, in her position? She's on the golf club committee.'

'Perhaps not, sir.' The policeman cleared his throat. 'If you don't want to speak to Mrs Rogers, why did you come here today?'

'I wanted to clear things up before I leave the area. You know, make a clean breast of things?'

'Where are you going?'

'I'm not too sure,' David admitted with an embarrassed smile. 'Jenny's a free spirit. We thought we'd hit the road and see where it takes us.'

'There will be one or two formalities to see to first.'

'I haven't done anything wrong, have I?' David demanded. 'I mean, you have my word I won't be asking Sally for any more money. I wasn't very good at it, actually. It was making me feel uncomfortable.'

'Why don't I fetch this famous jacket, and if it is yours you can have it back? Then once I've completed my incident report and you've signed it as a true copy, I don't think we'll need to detain you any longer, as long as you leave us with some forwarding details.'

A look of relief crossed David's face. 'Jenny's outside waiting for me. She wouldn't come in. Like me, she's brushed up against the authorities and, well . . . ' David shrugged. 'She doesn't like officialdom.'

'A sentiment shared by many citizens.' The policeman rose to his feet with a wry smile. 'Your tea's gone cold. Would you like another cup?'

David made a face. 'No, thank you. I just want to leave.'

'I won't be long.'

David leaned back in his chair and closed his eyes in relief. There would be no need to tell the police officer that he suspected Marian might be in danger from that madman of a delivery driver. He had attacked David viciously, and if David hadn't been so light on his feet he might not have got out of the barn alive. But Jenny and the open road were waiting for David, and that was where his future lay. He was finished with the past.

15

'I really don't understand where she can be.'

The sofa did not seem up to the challenge of supporting Ian's bulky frame. Marian had not seen him for a while and he had put on weight. Looking at him now, she could scarcely believe he had been her date on the night she had introduced him to her sister.

'You say she stayed at a bed and breakfast place on the way up here?'

'Yes.'

'Do you think she met up with anyone there?'

'She met the man who gave her these.' Marian held up one of Sally's pencils with her name stencilled in gold lettering. Ian hardly bothered to give it a glance.

'I didn't take her threat to leave me

seriously. I mean, it's not the first time she's walked out on our marriage. She's always been a drama queen.'

Marian feared she was in for a re-run of their previous conversation. She debated whether or not to tell Ian the full story behind Sally's arranged meeting with David Hicks.

'If you think she really is missing, I do have a local contact with the police,' Marian offered.

'You do?' Ian frowned.

'They called this number because a jacket was found abandoned on the beach.' Marian skated around the details. 'Sally wasn't here at the time.'

'Why did they call you?'

'There was a scrap of paper in the pocket with my parents' telephone number on it.'

'Do you think there's a connection between that and Sally's disappearance?' Ian asked.

'I don't know.' Marian's forehead creased in concern.

She and Sally had never been that

close and she couldn't help wondering if there was anything else her sister was hiding from her. It was proving to be a family trait — the keeping of secrets. Had Sally been as innocent as she professed of the crime for which she had been accused and sentenced? Marian knew little of the heartache she had caused their parents, but Sally had always been strong-willed. It wouldn't be difficult to imagine her sailing close to the wind for the thrill of it.

'I wouldn't want things to get too official.' Ian hesitated. 'Sally's always been impulsive, and if we report her disappearance to the law and then find out she's gone off just because she felt like it, we could be charged with wasting police time.'

'You haven't received any communication about her from anyone, have you?' Marian asked.

'What do you mean by anyone?'

'A third party, perhaps?'

'You're not talking ransom demands?'

Ian immediately picked up on the implied innuendo.

'I don't know what I'm talking,' Marian admitted.

'It wouldn't be the first time.'

'Are you saying Sally's been kidnapped in the past?' Marian gasped.

'There's this man, he said his name was Hicks.'

'David Hicks?'

'That's him. I caught him hanging around the house one day. Sally was out and he trotted out a trumped up story about being a friend of hers. He said she'd promised him some money. I didn't take to him and accused him of lying. We had words. Then he said something along the lines of I'd be sorry because he knew something about Sally that could ruin our marriage. How do you know him?'

'Sally mentioned his name.'

'Was he the man she was due to meet here?'

'Yes.' It seemed pointless to deny it.

'Why was he blackmailing her?'

Marian hesitated, then confessed, 'Sally has a police record.'

'And he thought that the threat of going public would split us up?' Ian gave a bitter laugh. 'We've done that without any help from him, but I tell you, if this Hicks person has harmed Sally, I won't be responsible for my actions.'

Marian felt a reluctant admiration for Ian. He had turned into a man she didn't much like anymore, but she admired his loyalty to Sally. 'It's so good to hear you say that,' she said, sagging against the back of the chair in relief.

'What else would you expect me to say? Sally's my wife. I love her.' Ian cleared his throat as if he were unused to such declarations.

'What was he like, David Hicks?' Marian asked to ease his embarrassment.

'A bit scruffy, hadn't shaved, dirty shirt. I think that's why I didn't trust him. You know how particular Sally is about her appearance.' Ian picked at a stray thread on a cushion cover. 'She didn't murder anyone, did she?' he asked in a quieter voice than usual.

'I think you ought to ask Sally that question.' Marian evaded a direct answer.

'I'm asking you,' Ian insisted.

'I don't know the full details.' Marian took a deep breath. 'All I'm prepared to say is it was a break-in that went wrong. As I understand it, the authorities needed to make an example of someone. One or two of those involved had influential parents who got them off the charge. Sally and this David Hicks didn't have any strings to pull and they went down.'

Ian now looked less pompous. 'I've been plucking up the courage to ask Sally about David Hicks, but things have been difficult between us recently and quite frankly I didn't want to rock the boat.'

'If you want to know what happened you will have to ask Sally,' Marian insisted.

'When we catch up with her I will,' Ian assured her. 'Any ideas as to what we do now? Have you had any thoughts as to where she might be?'

'She may be back in Essex,' Marian began.

'At this bed and breakfast place?'

'I don't think so, but I know she was trying to trace someone in that area.'

'It's not much to go on, is it?'

'It's all we have.'

They both jumped as there was a loud knock at the front door.

'Are you expecting visitors?' Ian asked.

Marian glanced through the curtains. A police car was parked on the verge outside.

* * *

'So there you have it, sir.' The police officer finished his story. 'I dropped by on the off chance that Miss Barr might still be here, because I thought she should know of the latest developments regarding the abandoned jacket on the beach. Mr Hicks has told us everything; and as no actual crime was committed, we haven't detained him.'

'What about the threats he made to my wife and the money he got off her?' Ian demanded. 'Don't they constitute a crime?'

'Mr Hicks has asked us to apologise to you and your family. I don't think you'll be hearing from him again, sir, so unless you want to take matters further I suggest we let the whole thing drop.'

'That's all very well, but he can't go round the countryside intimidating innocent members of the public.'

'I do appreciate that, sir but he has assured us he and Gypsy Jenny won't be remaining in the area, so I honestly don't think they pose any more of a threat to your wife.'

'Gypsy Jenny?' Ian repeated in disbelief. 'Who's she, a fairground turn?'

'I've made some enquiries about the lady, sir. It seems she is quite genuine and much respected amongst her circle of acquaintances. It's my professional opinion that we won't be having any more trouble from the gentleman concerned. Of course, if he should approach you or any of your family in the future, then I would suggest you get in touch with us immediately.'

'Why didn't you tell him that Sally's disappeared?' Marian demanded after the police officer had left.

'Perhaps I have over-reacted,' Ian admitted. 'As I told you, Sally and I have been going through a rough patch. I've been away a lot recently and you know how Sally hates being on her own. If she thought David Hicks might try and approach her in my absence, maybe it spooked her and she's decided to lie low until things blow over.'

'Sally's not the type to spook easily, and surely she would have left a note of some sort if she was going away to stay with a friend for a few days?'

'She didn't know when to expect me back.'

'She could have left a message on

your mobile phone.'

'No she couldn't,' Ian mumbled, not looking Marian in the eye.

'Why not?'

'I replaced my mobile phone. I lost the old one somewhere and I haven't got round to telling her the new number.'

Marian frowned. There was something about Ian's explanation that didn't ring true. 'Are you telling me the absolute truth?'

Ian opened his mouth as if to protest, then appeared to think better of it. 'I had a relationship with a female colleague,' he confessed. 'I was feeling low after yet another bust-up with Sally. We were away at a conference, staying in a country house hotel and enjoying a drink in the bar before dinner. I flirted a bit with her. She was young and pretty and laughed at my jokes. One thing led to another. It didn't mean a thing, but afterwards she sent me a few indiscreet texts. I deleted them, but the situation was a bit uncomfortable for a time. So much so, I thought it wise to dispose of my old mobile and get a new one. You know, in case Sally read the texts?'

Marian knew she had been right not to like Ian. He professed to love Sally, but he wasn't above having a dalliance with a female colleague.

'Anyway, that's why Sally hasn't been in touch with me.' Ian looked at Marian expectantly, but when she said nothing, admitted, 'Our marriage is on borrowed time.'

'Then as you're not going to report her disappearance, the best thing you can do is to go home and wait for her to contact you.' Marian wanted to create as much space as possible between them. His presence made her uneasy.

Ian glanced at his designer watch. 'It's late.'

Marian's heart sank. She could tell by the expression on his face that he wasn't going to be easy to get rid of.

'You're welcome to stay the night.' She issued a reluctant invitation, glad there was a lock on her bedroom door.

'What say I take you out to dinner and then we come back here and crash out? I could use the sofa.'

'There's no need for that.' Marian straightened her back and dismissed her fears as a tired over-reaction to the situation. She could deal with a bit of unwanted attention should Ian start discussing intimate nightcaps. 'We converted a downstairs room into a bedroom for my father. You can sleep there.'

'Fine. I'll do that. If you want to freshen up before we go out I'm going to grab forty winks.'

Despite Marian's earlier fears, Ian proved an entertaining dinner companion. With his unerring instinct for the good things in life, he managed to locate a local brasserie, where they enjoyed an excellent meal.

'They've got a piano,' he said as he and Marian lingered over coffee in the adjacent lounge.

'You're not going to suggest I play for

my supper?' Marian joked.

'Why not? No one's using it.'

'It's probably out of tune.'

Before Marian could stop him, Ian signalled to the coffee waiter. After a brief huddled conversation with the manager, he was back by her side.

'The management would be delighted to hear you play. The regular pianist is off sick.'

'I don't normally do this sort of thing,' Marian attempted to explain to the manager who had come forward to welcome her.

'I did not realise who you are, Miss Barr. It would be an honour to have you play for our guests. My wife is a volunteer on the committee helping to arrange your charity concert. Perhaps we could have a sneak preview of the programme?'

'Mr Pascal and I haven't decided on our schedule yet.'

'Of course, I understand, but are you sure I can't tempt you to play if only for a little while? You are a local celebrity.'

Looks were now being cast in Marian's direction and one or two people began to recognise her. She glanced at the small piano in the corner of the room, aware that she had missed her practice for several days now.

Someone began to clap and soon everyone took up the applause. One or two of the diners actually stood up.

'There,' the manager indicated his satisfaction, 'you can't let your public down.'

Seated at the piano, Marian began to play; and as was usual when she was engaged in the activity she most loved in this world, she completely forgot the time. When she finally looked at the wall clock, she realised with an embarrassed start that she had been seated at the piano for over two hours and that the brasserie was empty of diners.

'I'm so sorry,' she apologised to the hovering waiters. 'You must be desperate to get home.'

'Not at all,' the headwaiter assured

her. 'We didn't have time to listen while we were serving, but after people started to leave we were free to enjoy your performance. Thank you so much for a wonderful evening.'

The waiters now applauded.

'I suppose we had better leave too.' Ian finished his brandy and rose to his feet. An attendant came forward with their coats.

'We hope to see you again soon,' the manager said as he bade them goodbye at the door.

'I'll be back with Mr Pascal,' Marian assured him as they made their way to Ian's car.

'It's getting cold again,' Ian complained. 'No one would think spring was round the corner. Is it always so chilly in this part of the world?'

'Don't knock it,' Marian chided. 'There's nothing like the start of a new year in the fens.'

'I'll take your word for it.' Ian shivered.

'Soft southerner,' she teased.

A quarter of an hour later, they approached Hatpin Cottage.

'There's a dedicated parking area round the corner,' Marian indicated. 'If you drive on a bit I'll show you where.'

Ian buried his nose in his scarf. 'To protect myself from the elements,' he explained, catching Marian's look of surprise as they began to trudge back down the lane. He linked his arm through hers. 'Shared bodily warmth. You don't mind, do you? You know, you're looking very lovely tonight.'

Ian was being far too tactile for comfort and Marian's earlier fears resurfaced. She had absolutely no intention of being another of his little liaisons that 'didn't mean a thing'. Very firmly, she unhooked her arm from his and began looking in her bag for the front door key.

'Here, let me help you,' Ian coaxed in a seductive voice as he moved in close again.

'I can manage,' Marian insisted, pushing him away.

'Do you never wonder what might have happened if Sally hadn't come between us that night all those years ago?' he asked.

'No, never.' Marian had been right to trust her inner instinct. The sooner Ian was back home in Berkshire, the better.

'I can't help thinking we'd have made a good team. You're a successful professional woman, unlike Sally.'

'May I remind you you're talking about my sister, your wife?'

'You had those waiters eating out of your hand tonight.' With a yelp of surprise, Ian toppled backwards. 'What was that for?' he demanded as he extricated himself from the holly bush at the gate. 'You elbowed me in the ribs.'

'I think perhaps you'd better drive back to Berkshire tonight.' Marian thrust her key into the lock.

'Well, I don't. I'm tired. I've been drinking brandy and you offered me a bed for the night. Remember? We could share a nightcap before we settle down and relive old times. What do you say?'

Ian moved in close again. Neither of them noticed a dark figure emerge silently from the shadows. 'I don't think you heard what Miss Barr said,' he spoke in a cold, clear voice.

'Who are you?' Ian snapped angrily.

'Georges Pascal.'

'So you're the famous fiancé,' Ian sneered.

'And you, I take it, are Ian Rogers, her brother-in-law?'

'What if I am? I'm entitled to be here.' Ian was now sounding belligerent. 'If you must know, Marian and I have been discussing family business.'

'From what I heard, your business discussion would appear to be over.'

'I've been reading about your antics in the newspaper,' Ian blustered. 'You needn't think there's anything going on between us.'

'I'm very pleased to hear it. Now, don't let us detain you any longer.'

'I'm staying the night.'

'No you're not,' Georges insisted.

'Marian's offered me a bed.'

'I'm sure there's a comfortable hotel somewhere in the area, so why don't you take yourself off before you outstay your welcome?'

Ian hesitated; then, scowling at the pair of them, he turned on his heel, and without another word disappeared into the darkness.

16

'You can't hold me here.' Sally's eyes flashed a dangerous depth of green. She tilted her chin in challenge and glared into an equally antagonistic pair of brown eyes. 'I've done nothing wrong.'

'Breaking and entering is a crime.'

'I didn't break in. The door was open.'

'Your sort are all the same. Think the law doesn't apply to you.'

'This is a business, isn't it? People are allowed to walk in.'

'Shut up. I hate mouthy women.'

'Why am I trussed up like a turkey?'

'I said shut up.' Brian delivered a stinging slap across her face. 'In future you'll only speak when spoken to. Understand?'

Sally could feel her eye beginning to close up.

The man's next words chilled her

spine. 'You're Marian Barr's sister, aren't you? Answer me,' he yelled.

She made a noise at the back of her throat.

'Thought so. People think I'm thick, but I'm not. Nothing to say?' He lowered his face to hers. It was the most evil experience of Sally's life.

'Who are you?' she croaked.

'Brian Bartholomew at your service.' He sketched a small bow.

Sally's blood froze. Bartholomew — that was the name of the people who adopted Marian's son.

'And I've made it my business to know everything there is to know about your sister.'

'You can't be her son.' Again, Sally's voice gave out.

'You're right,' Brian admitted. 'I'm not. I'm Peter's brother.'

Sally coughed to clear the blockage in her throat. 'What are you after?'

'Money.'

'Why?'

'Because Peter was the baby she gave

away. She didn't want him.'

'She loved him so much she cried for weeks afterwards. She told me.'

'Then she can ease her conscience and prove her love for Peter by paying up. And my silence doesn't come cheap.'

'Love isn't about money.'

'Nobody's ever loved me.'

'That's nonsense.'

Brian seemed to have forgotten his earlier threat to Sally to keep quiet. 'I made sure that weirdo in the tweed jacket didn't stake his claim.' His eyes began to look angry again.

'Who?' Sally frowned.

'The one at the station.'

'What about him?'

Even though her head was throbbing from the strain, Sally knew it was vital to keep Brian talking. She had to build up a relationship.

'He was after the same thing. Not now he isn't.'

'You killed him?'

'No idea.' Brian dismissed Sally's

question as if it were of no importance.

She lowered her eyes, not wanting him to see the hate reflected in them. She had to get out of here before Brian decided to kill her too. She sneaked a glance at the emergency exit. It was blocked by an old filing cabinet. The only way out was the doorway to the yard, and Brian was blocking it.

'Your sister's past had to catch up with her one day, and that day has come.'

Sally tugged at the rope securing her to a wooden chair. She couldn't believe how stupid she had been to come back and start poking around the depot, especially after one of the drivers had threatened to see her off the premises when she tried to ask questions. She should have taken his advice and stayed away. Instead, after speaking to the receptionist, she had driven into town. With the local bank closed for two weeks and funds running low, and her mobile credit cut off just as she tried to telephone Marian, Sally decided to give up on her quest and drive home.

Back in Berkshire there had still been no word from Ian. What she did find was a picture of Georges Pascal staring at her from the front page of the newspaper. He had made the headlines after walking out on rehearsals in Salzburg. The official reason given by his agent was that he was missing his fiancée.

Sally didn't believe a word of it. Something must have happened to make him take such drastic action, and Sally knew what it was. He had found out about Marian's past. Realising they were all getting in a bit deep, she decided to let Marian sort things out. Sally had enough troubles of her own. Her priority was Ian and their marriage, and it was time she started acting like a wife.

Going through Ian's jackets to take to the cleaners, she came across his mobile phone in one of the pockets. No wonder he wasn't answering his calls, she thought, tossing it onto the bed.

It signalled an incoming message. She snatched it up and frowned. The text appeared to be from a female colleague and there was no mistaking its meaning. Sally scrolled down the call history. It wasn't the first by any means.

Feeling sick, she sank onto the bed. In an instant she decided what she was going to do. If Ian loved her, he would come looking for her; otherwise their marriage was over.

She was going back to Essex. At least Marian would never desert her.

★ ★ ★

Wearing dark clothing to make sure she couldn't be seen, Sally had slipped through an open door round the back of the warehouse. It led into a storeroom. A man had come in unexpectedly and before she'd had time to react, he had quickly overcome her and tied her to a chair. Now she was beginning to realise she was seriously out of her league, and that her actions had been foolhardy beyond belief. Brian's eyes were glazed with power and another emotion that made Sally tremble. She'd seen it once before when she'd been serving her sentence. There'd been a fight, and an inmate with a serious grudge against Sally had attacked her with a broken bottle. There had been murder in her assailant's eyes that day, and Brian was looking at her with the same expression.

'You can't keep me here.' Sally's swollen eye had now completely closed, but she was determined to show no fear.

'I can do what I like with you,' Brian informed her in an unnaturally calm voice that told Sally he was in control and he knew it. 'You're my prisoner.'

'My husband will come looking for me. So will Marian.'

'But they won't know where to find you, will they?'

A telephone rang in the far corner of the storeroom. Brian muttered something under his breath before answering the call. 'Can't you deal with it?' he said, after listening for a few moments. There was another pause and the sound of an angry voice down the line. Brian yanked the cable out of the wall.

'I wouldn't want you trying to contact any of your fancy friends in my absence,' he said.

'Where are you going?' Sally demanded.

'Boss isn't best pleased I wasn't in the control centre. If I lose my job it'll be your fault.' He turned to her with a sneer. 'I might come back. I might not. I might leave you to rot. Whatever, you'll have plenty of time to think about your fate.'

The sound of the key being turned in the lock was a death knell to Sally's hope of escape. A naked bulb dangled from a wire above her head. At least Brian hadn't thought to turn off the light. She tugged in frustration at the ropes binding her wrists, but they didn't give. It wouldn't do to dwell on how idiotic she had been. She had to escape, but how?

Would the receptionist on the main desk hear her if she shouted for help? Would she even come to her aid? Sally sensed she was soft on Brian. His boyish looks were enough to set an impressionable female's pulse racing. He could feed her any story she liked and the girl would believe him. In any other circumstances Sally would have felt sorry for her. She could have told her not to waste her time. The Brian Bartholomews of this world only used people to their own advantage. They didn't fall in love with the likes of homely receptionists.

'Help!' Sally bellowed at the top of her voice, figuring there had to be someone around to hear her in a busy depot.

There was no reply. She had no idea of the time, but by her reckoning it had to be late afternoon. She had waited until after lunch to gain her illegal access, and that had been several hours ago. She tugged at her restraints again, but they still didn't give. Mustering all her strength, she bumped her chair across the stone floor. The walls were built of rough stone. She had seen enough films to know there was always a jagged edge that acted like a razor blade in these circumstances. If she could just sever the rope binding her wrists, she could make her escape.

Her throat wobbled as she thought of Ian and the argument they had had what now seemed like months ago before he had left for his business trip. Would he think she had left him for real this time? Was that why he had taken up with a colleague?

'Think positive.' Sally ground out the words and did her best to keep upbeat. If Ian didn't come looking for her, Marian would eventually, but Sally feared her sister's attempts to find her might be too late.

For a moment panic almost got the better of her. She bit down the urge to scream. Now was not the time for hysterics. Now was the time to keep a clear head, even if she could only view the world through one eye.

She winced as something sharp jabbed her hip, then remembered she had thrust one of her new pencils into the pocket of her jeans. Why couldn't it have been something useful like a penknife?

Sally had another go at bumping her chair across the floor towards the wall. Her recent skiing holiday had left her reasonably toned and fit, and she was making good progress when one of the chair legs cracked beneath her weight and she went crashing to the floor.

After that everything went black.

Sally gasped as the contents of a glass of cold water hit her in the face. She had difficulty focusing on the face in front of her before the mists began to clear.

'Your fancy friends wouldn't want to know you now. You're a mess.' Brian wrinkled his nose. 'And you smell.'

He hauled her and the broken chair off the floor.

'It won't balance,' Sally shouted at

him as she wobbled against a discarded desk.

'Tough. You should have stayed where I put you.' His breath smelt of stale coffee as he leaned over her.

Sally suppressed another shudder. 'I've never done anything any man's told me to do.' She didn't bother to lower her voice. The more she shouted, she figured, the more chance there was that someone would overhear.

'You'll learn to obey me or pay the consequences.' Brian's smile revealed his ugly teeth.

'No way.' Sally shook droplets of water off her fringe. The dousing had revived her spirits and eased the pain in her eye. With renewed strength, she tugged at the bonds holding her.

'I like it when females struggle,' Brian replied in a deceptively mild voice, leering at her as he spoke. He licked his moist lips. 'Especially when they're in bondage. It spices things up.'

Dear God, what had she walked into? As well as a stalker he was a pervert.

'You're going to have to let me go.'

'You don't tell me what to do. Nobody tells me what to do. I'm Brian Bartholomew,' he ranted.

Sally realised if she wasn't careful she'd push him over the top.

'You're my ticket to the big time. You are Marian Barr's sister.'

'Then it won't do any good killing me,' she said in a desperate effort to get him to see sense.

'You're right.' He looked down at her. 'But I could send her one of your fingers in the post. She and that husband of yours would be bound to recognise your rings, wouldn't you say?'

Sally's insides liquefied. 'Please, no,' she whimpered.

'I like it when you beg. Beg some more,' Brian urged.

'I need the ladies' room, urgently. Please?' It nearly killed Sally to summon up a smile, and she suspected it was more of a grimace, but Brian looked the type of male who would believe she found him attractive. She had to play a dangerous game if she wanted to get out of this hellhole alive.

'You think we could make music together? Share the spoils? You get Marian to pay up, then we could hit the high life together. I could show you a good time.'

'Maybe,' Brian acknowledged.

'That's if your girlfriend doesn't get jealous.'

'I don't have a girlfriend.'

'What about the one on the reception desk? I reckon she's sweet on you.'

'Sara?' Brian's lips curled in an ugly twist. 'She's fine at baking cookies but I like my women edgy.'

'Then what are we waiting for? Marian's loaded. With me as your bargaining tool you could double your demand.'

'No funny business,' Brian warned, releasing her bonds.

Sally rubbed her raw wrists and wriggled her hands and feet to get her circulation going. It had worked.

'There's a toilet block out the back of

the main building.' He pulled her to her feet. Sally winced as pins and needles shot up her leg. 'Cramp,' she gasped.

Brian clamped a hand over her mouth and pinioned the back of her body to the front of his. 'Don't make a sound or you'll regret it,' he said as he frogmarched her towards the exit.

Sally stumbled, playing for time.

'Watch where you're going,' he growled in her ear.

She wriggled in his hold; then as they neared the door, she jabbed her elbow into his stomach, winding him. He doubled over in pain. Sally took off.

She didn't know where she was going, but she did know there should be someone around in the main depot. In the distance she could see lights arcing the sky. Mustering every ounce of strength she possessed and screaming like a banshee, she headed towards them, ignoring the sound of pounding feet behind her.

17

'My meeting was cancelled after I arrived in New York,' Georges explained. 'The backers have withdrawn their financial support for the proposed tour. I caught the red eye straight back to London. Your concierge told me you were in Suffolk, so here I am. Why was Ian here?' he demanded.

Marian and Georges were seated in the kitchen after Ian had abandoned his plans to sleep over.

'We don't know where Sally is. No one's seen her for ages.'

'That is not your concern.' Georges did not look very interested in the problem.

'She's my sister, Georges.'

'And Ian is her husband. She is his responsibility. He should take better care of his wife. From what I overheard, he does not seem unduly concerned for her welfare.'

Anxious to avoid a scene, Marian turned the conversation around by suggesting, 'Now you are here, you can help me look for her.'

Georges stifled a yawn. 'I am suffering from jet lag. I do not intend looking for anyone. We can talk in the morning, but right now as I appear to have been twenty-four hours without sleep, my body clock suggests we go to bed.'

★   ★   ★

After a late breakfast they took their coffee outside onto the terrace to enjoy the morning sun. Georges settled down in a battered garden seat that had seen better days. 'I hope this thing is safe.' He tested his weight on it. 'Why we have to sit here when we could just as well have been indoors in the warm is beyond me.'

'You've spent far too much time cooped up in stuffy aircraft.' Marian sat opposite him. 'Your complexion is suffering.'

'Pale is interesting.' Georges raised his face to the sun and closed his eyes.

Marian hid a smile. It had been a stroke of brilliance hitting on Georges' vanity. 'Look.' Marian pointed to the overgrown flowerbed.

Georges opened his eyes. 'Now what?' he asked lazily.

'Green shoots coming through.'

'Should I be excited?'

'Yes, you should.'

Georges leaned forward and caressed the back of Marian's hand with the rough patch of his thumb. 'You are the only thing that excites me at the moment. Yet you look so demure sitting there,' he teased, 'with your blouse buttoned up to your neck and wearing a pink cardigan decorated with daisies.'

Marian suspected her complexion was turning as pink as her cardigan. Georges' lovemaking had reawakened her sexual appetite, something she never thought to experience again after

Valentin. Last night she had clung to him hungrily until they both fell into an exhausted sleep just before dawn.

'We have things to talk about.' She tugged at her hand, imprisoned by Georges' fingers. 'We really do need to track Sally down.'

'This sister of yours is beginning to sound like a nuisance. I'm not sure I like her.'

'You'll like Sally,' Marian insisted. 'Everybody does.'

'Is that why you haven't introduced her to me before now?'

'What do you mean?'

'You are scared that I will find her more attractive than you?'

'Of course not.' Marian wished her words didn't sound quite so unconvincing.

'I can see in your eyes that my suspicions are correct,' Georges crowed. 'You need not worry. I have broken a professional date, almost sacrificed my career and flown back across the Atlantic at a moment's notice for you. That is something I have never done for another woman. Does that satisfy you?'

'It does,' Marian replied with a slow smile.

'If you don't believe me, I could make love to you now to prove it.' His words deepened Marian's blush.

'No,' she protested.

'We shall have to get married soon,' Georges said with a sigh. 'I want to introduce you to everyone as my wife and I want to make love to you whenever I wish.'

'Not until we've found Sally.'

'Very well, back to this wretched sister of yours. Now, think hard,' Georges instructed Marian, already switching priorities with his characteristic intensity of focus. 'Where would she go?'

'I know she hasn't gone off with David Hicks, the man she was here to meet. The police gave me a written note from him. He says he's sorry and he won't be bothering her again.'

'Then where else can she be?'

Something was niggling the back of Marian's mind. Something she was struggling to remember.

'Speak to me,' Georges prompted.

'Essex.' Marian sat up straight.

'Where?'

'Peggy Bartholomew mentioned it and Sally dialled an Essex number before she left the cottage. I know because I checked.'

'Who do you know in Essex?'

'Brian Bartholomew, Peggy's son, works as a delivery driver for a firm in Essex.'

'He is the one who has been sending you unpleasant messages and making threatening telephone calls?'

Marian nodded. 'I think so.'

'Why would Sally be going after him?'

'Because of the bad weather, he was forced to take shelter in that barn where we found the duck.'

'Wait. Hold on a moment.' Georges frowned. 'I do not know anything about any duck.'

Marian rose to her feet. She was back a few moments later clutching the little yellow toy. Georges took it from her trembling hands. 'See?' Marian turned it over. 'I recognised it instantly.'

'I love you.' Georges read aloud the words scratched on the bottom. 'You wrote this?'

Marian nodded. 'I smuggled it into Peter's baby blanket before they took him away.' Her voice shook.

'My poor darling.' Georges' blue eyes were full of compassion. 'Your life has been filled with so much hurt. I will make it up to you, I promise. There will be no more tears when we are married. Together we will have lots of children and you will be free to love them as much as you wish.'

Marian put the duck down on the wooden table with a wistful smile. Peter was only a part of her life for such a short time, and she was sure Peggy had been a loving mother to him, but she would never forget her firstborn no matter how many children she and

Georges produced.

'Let me get this straight. You found this duck in the barn where we took shelter?'

Marian nodded.

'That is why you were so shocked? I was right to suspect it wasn't the cold making you shiver.'

'I suppose Brian must have dropped it. David Hicks was sheltering with him. There was some sort of scuffle or disagreement, because the police told me David banged his head and lost his memory as a result of a fall or a blow. He was found wandering about the beach by a gypsy and she tended his wounds until his memory came back. That's when he went to the police and confessed everything.'

'I used to think the English were very unemotional people. I was wrong. They can be a very hot-blooded race, full of passion and life.' There was a glint in Georges' blue eyes as he added, 'you, my darling were my first proof of that.'

'Sally must have discovered something and hared off to Essex,' Marian said, determined not to be sidetracked.

'Without a word to anyone?'

'It's the sort of thing she would do.'

'How long has she been missing?'

'I'm not sure.'

'Haven't you got any leads?'

'Only Peggy Bartholomew,' Marian admitted.

'Call her.' Georges snapped his fingers impatiently.

The telephone was ringing as Marian went indoors.

'Ian?' she greeted her brother-in-law reluctantly. 'Have you any news of Sally?'

'I keep trying her number but there's no reply. I've tried our home number too but she's not there either,' he replied in a crisp voice that held none of the warmth of the previous evening.

'I think it's possible she may be in Essex.'

'What on earth would she be doing

there?' There was now surprise in Ian's voice.

'It's just an idea I've had. I was about to telephone a contact.'

'I'm beginning to think perhaps we should contact the police,' Ian admitted. 'How long does someone have to go missing before they take you seriously?'

'I don't know,' Marian answered.

'Is Georges staying on?'

'For a while.'

'Then I think the best thing is for me to go home in case Sally tries to contact me there. I'll keep in touch.' He cut the call, not giving Marian the chance to reply.

Peggy Bartholomew answered immediately. It was as if she had been waiting by the telephone.

18

Georges shifted in the passenger seat of Marian's car and looked out of the rain-lashed window. 'The view is uninspiring. I would not wish to make music here.'

'Have you never heard of Southend-on-Sea?' Marian asked. 'It boasts the longest pier in the world. In its time it has hosted all sorts of activities.'

'What sort of activities?'

'End-of-the-pier comedians, dance shows, light entertainment for the trippers.'

'You're not thinking of appearing there as one of these activities?' Georges asked, a scandalised look on his face.

'Why not?' Marian teased him. 'Don't you think I'd be a hit? We could have a bit of a sing-song, dance along the pier wearing hats displaying rude slogans, then go for a fish and chip supper afterwards.'

'It doesn't sound very dignified to me.'

'It isn't, but it's huge fun. You must try it some time.'

'Concentrate.' Georges clung onto the dashboard as Marian swerved to avoid an oncoming vehicle. 'Do you have to drive so violently?' He swivelled round and tried to apologise to the gesticulating driver they had narrowly missed.

'Did you see what it was?' Marian asked in an excited voice.

'Of course I did. It was a delivery van.'

'Not any delivery van.' She snatched up a scrap of paper. 'Look.'

Georges read the details Marian had scrawled down after her telephone conversation with Peggy Bartholomew, when the older woman had told Marian where her son worked.

'The same details were painted on the side of the van that just passed us,' she shouted at a puzzled-looking Georges. 'We're getting close.'

'I'm not sure this was a good idea.' Georges scrunched up her note. 'We should have let the police deal with this.'

'And do what? No crime has been committed. There's nothing to go on apart from our suspicions.'

'That's as may be, but you've no idea what you could be getting into.'

'My sister wouldn't disappear without a word to anyone.'

'You said it is exactly the sort of thing she would do.'

'I admit she can be a bit unpredictable at times, but she's a mother of two daughters. She wouldn't abandon them.'

'She is also a wife. Her husband, not you, should be scouring the Essex countryside looking for her. You know she's probably run off with another man.'

'That's not true.'

'It's what I would do in her place. Ian no longer loves her.'

'We don't know that.'

'He was making overtures to you the other night.'

'There it is.' Marian slammed on the brakes, causing Georges to again grab the dashboard. The car slued to an angled halt.

'I wish you wouldn't keep doing that,' he protested, adding a violent volley of Eastern European as he massaged the back of his neck. 'If you're not careful we'll get arrested for dangerous driving. On second thought, that's not a bad idea. At least the police would listen to us then. What is it?' Georges demanded, looking in the direction of Marian's pointing finger.

'The depot.' She made gestures at the Victorian iron railing gates. 'And this is Railway Approach. We're here. Peggy said it was a converted warehouse by the old station.'

'Right.' Georges stopped rubbing his neck. 'What do you suggest we do?'

'We drive in and make enquiries.'

'Now?'

'That's what we came for.'

'Exactly how do we go about it? You'll have to forgive my ignorance. I don't have experience of delivery depots.'

'We walk through the doors. We greet the receptionist nice and politely, then you use your charm on the girl on the desk. She's bound to be putty in your hands once you smile at her. Most women are.'

'And if it's a male member of staff on duty? I hope you're not going to suggest I use my smile on a man?'

'Then I'll have a go,' Marian replied as she parked the car in a vacant slot. 'Come on.'

Still grumbling, Georges climbed out of the passenger seat. 'I thought you said spring was on the way.' He turned up his coat collar.

'For someone who comes from a cold place, you don't do cold weather very well, do you?' Marian responded, pushing Georges towards the bright lights of the reception area. 'On you go.'

Red lights were flashing on a switchboard as they pushed open the large glass doors. A harassed female was busy answering two calls at once. 'Sorry,' she apologised in a hurry, 'the boss is away and his cover has been delayed. I'll see what I can do, sir.' She waved an acknowledgement to Georges and Marian before turning her attention back to the switchboard to deal with another call.

Marian took the chance to look round. The reception area was no different from hundreds of others. A huge notice board in one corner listed various company announcements and activities. There was a water cooler by the door and a potted plant that could have done with a drink. The plastic chairs were functional and obviously well-used. Several discarded coffee cups littered the floor.

Georges nudged Marian and pointed to a CCTV screen in a far corner of the room. 'Do you recognise him?' he pointed to a driver getting out of a cab.

'It's not Brian Bartholomew,' she replied, keeping her voice low.

'How do you know?' he hissed back at her. 'I thought you hadn't met him.'

'I saw a photo at Peggy's. He's overweight, with floppy, dirty blond hair, and he's in his twenties. That driver is much older.'

'Jack.' The female receptionist greeted him with a smile of relief as he lumbered through the doors. 'You couldn't help out, could you?'

'No problem.' He strolled over to the main control centre. 'On your own?'

'Brian was supposed to be on duty. I don't know where he is.'

Georges bit down a yelp as Marian nudged him in the ribs. 'Did you get that?' she hissed.

'He had a row with the boss yesterday and didn't turn up this morning,' the receptionist was explaining. 'You haven't seen him, have you?'

'Sorry, can't help, but you know Brian. He's not the most reliable card in the pack. I've heard he's got a girl in every town from here to London. He's probably gone off with one of them.'

'I'm sure that's not true,' the receptionist replied, a fleeting look of hurt crossing her face.

'Maybe not. Anyway, leave the drivers' console to me. You go and see to our visitors.'

Pasting a professional smile on her face, the receptionist turned to Georges and Marian. 'What can I do to help you, sir?'

'Sara, is it?' Georges inspected her name badge.

Marian hid a smile as she watched the girl visibly melt under his famous charm. 'Yes, sir.'

'Then I'm sure you can help us.'

Sara blinked. 'Aren't you Georges Pascal?' she squeaked back at him with an excited look in her eyes.

'Yes, I am.'

'I'm such a fan of yours,' Sara gushed.

Georges stepped back in surprise. Marian always found this side of his character endearing. On the podium when he was conducting an orchestra he had a huge ego, and enjoyed the charisma of being the person everyone was looking at, but she could tell he was sincerely touched by this girl's delight at meeting him.

'You have heard of me?'

'My mother's a fan, too.'

'Is she indeed?'

'We always watch the television when you're on. I like the operas best. They're so romantic, even if half of them end sadly.' Sara sighed happily. 'Mum will never believe me when I tell her you've been here.'

Sara's eyes nearly popped out of her head as Marian joined them at the desk. 'You're Marian Barr.'

'I am indeed.'

'You and Mr Pascal are an item, aren't you?'

Marian showed her the ruby and diamond engagement ring Georges had presented to her when he had got down on one knee to propose, much to

Marian's embarrassment, in the middle of a restaurant packed with diners.

'It's beautiful,' Sara said enviously. 'Wish I had one.'

'Don't you have a boyfriend?' Georges asked.

Sara pulled a face. 'Not anyone special.'

'In that case I insist you bring your mother to our charity gala performance.'

'I don't think we would be able to afford tickets; and even if we could, isn't there a waiting list?'

'As our guests,' Georges insisted.

'Really?' Sara was by now ecstatic. 'I've been reading about the plans for the concert in the newspaper but I never in a million years thought I'd be able to go. Wait until I tell Mum. Excuse me.' She looked over her shoulder as the switchboard again sprang into life. 'Duty calls.'

'Well done, you,' Marian murmured to Georges, trying not to move her lips. 'She's eating out of your hand.'

'I have done the spade work,' Georges replied. 'Now it's your turn. I hope you can come up with something good to explain our reason for being here.'

Marian hushed him, then wrinkled her forehead in concentration, wondering what excuse she could think up to explain their presence in a transport depot.

'Do you want something delivered?' Sara was back at the desk.

Marian took a deep breath and decided to go for the truth. 'The thing is, we are looking for my sister.'

Sara blinked at her. 'I'm the only female on the staff. Your sister doesn't work here.'

'We think she may have been in the area recently. Would you remember her? She's in her late thirties, blonde-haired, tanned. Name of Sally Rogers.'

'She's not the lady enquiring about removal expenses in Suffolk, is she?' Sara asked after a few moments' thought.

'That sounds like her.' Marian did her best to quell her excitement.

'She mentioned something about your parents' cottage and that you were clearing it out?'

'That's right.' Marian caught her breath and waited for Sara to go on.

'I told her Suffolk was a bit off our beaten track and that we don't do house clearances, but to contact us again if she couldn't find anyone closer and more suitable and I'd see what we could do. Why are you looking for her?'

'My fiancée's sister is rather forget-ful.' Georges came to Marian's rescue as she turned to him for help. 'We haven't been able to contact her by mobile phone. We think she may have forgotten to recharge it, and as her husband is away she's not at home at the moment. It's been a day or two since we heard from her and we need to get in touch. We knew she was thinking of contacting your company and we wondered if perhaps she was staying in the area.' Marian threw him a grateful look.

'I see.' Sara, too, seemed satisfied by his explanation. 'Well, I'm sorry I can't be of more help. She didn't leave an address with us.'

'Would this Brian you mentioned know anything about her?' Marian did her best to keep her voice as neutral as possible.

'Brian?' Sara looked mystified.

'The one who's not turned up for work today?'

'She doesn't know him, does she?' Sara began to look less amenable.

'I thought he might have been on duty when Sally called.'

'He was,' Sara admitted. 'Actually, he seemed annoyed when I mentioned her. He told me the next time she made contact I was to tell her to stop bothering us.'

'Did he indeed?' Georges said. 'Hardly good customer relations.'

'She's not one of his lady friends, is she?' Sara asked. 'You know, the ones

Jack was talking about?'

'Sally's a married woman,' Marian assured her.

'And this Brian has taken off without telling anyone?' Georges asked.

'The boss wasn't best pleased with him yesterday and gave him an official warning after he sneaked off for a cigarette and left the control room unmanned. Brian's always done his own thing. He disappeared for ages during the snowstorm, saying he was stranded somewhere,' Sara said. 'Now I come to think of it . . . ' she chewed her lower lip.

'What is it?' Marian demanded.

She made a gesture of annoyance as the switchboard cut in again.

'It's going very well, isn't it?' Georges raised his eyebrows.

'We know Sally was here,' Marian replied, 'but we don't know where she is now.'

'Sorry about that.' Sara smiled at Georges as she came back to the counter. 'Where was I?'

'You were going to tell us something else about my sister?'

'That's right.' She frowned. 'I thought it odd at the time, but it may be nothing. Now where did I put it?' Sara began looking through the contents of the shelves under the counter. 'I found it on the floor of the old storeroom. It's hardly ever used these days. That's what surprised me. I've got the keys and one of the drivers told me the door was open. It shouldn't have been, so I went down to lock it. That's when I found it on the floor. Ah, here it is. You did say your sister's first name was Sally, didn't you?'

'I did,' Marian replied.

'Is this hers?'

Marian looked down at the object Sara rolled across the counter towards her. It was a pencil, and emblazoned in gold lettering was the name Sally.

19

'Our colleagues have contacted David Hicks,' the police officer informed Marian. 'The bad weather delayed him and this Gypsy Jenny so they haven't left the area. 'Your sister isn't with them.'

'You're not listening to me.' Marian's voice was a hysterical shriek. 'Brian Bartholomew's got her.'

'We don't know that.'

'He didn't turn up for work this morning. We know my sister was in the storeroom; the receptionist found one of her pencils on the floor. What more proof do you want? And your records will show Brian attacked David Hicks in that barn. He was stalking me and he's kidnapped my sister.'

Georges squeezed Marian's hand in an attempt to calm her down. 'What Miss Barr says is true, officer. I received a telephone call from this Brian person, telling me my fiancée was having an affair. I was so worried I immediately flew back from Salzburg.'

'Yes, I did read about that incident in the paper, sir.' The tone of the officer's voice suggested he would have expected that sort of behaviour from someone like Georges. 'Very foolhardy, I thought. As for the business with the pencil, we know Mrs Rogers visited the depot. She could have dropped it anywhere on the premises. It's hardly evidence. I gather from the receptionist she was making enquiries about some removal work regarding your parents' effects?'

'What would be the point of coming all this way?' Marian demanded. 'It doesn't make sense.'

'We've spoken to Mr Rogers and he tells us he and his wife were undergoing something of a trial separation.'

'What's that got to do with anything? Sally's been kidnapped by that monster and you're sitting there asking stupid questions.'

'We have to explore every possibility,' the police officer replied calmly. 'I also understand from her husband that your sister was something of an independent spirit and that it wasn't unusual for her to go off like this. She has done it before hasn't she?'

'Yes, but . . . '

'In our experience, in over ninety per cent of cases people who disappear don't want to be found, and most of those who do take off without telling anyone usually turn up safe and sound eventually.'

'So you're going to do nothing?'

'We're in touch with Mr Rogers.'

'But he's miles away in Berkshire.'

'He is the next of kin and I think the best thing you can do, Miss Barr, is leave everything to us.' The expression on his face softened. 'I can understand your concern, but there's no need to worry. I'm sure your sister will turn up safe and sound.'

Out in the car park, Marian turned on Georges. 'What are we going to do?'

'You heard the police, my darling. What can we do?'

'I'm not sitting around waiting for Sally to get murdered.'

'Perhaps she was only poking around in that storeroom and that was when she dropped the pencil; or maybe someone borrowed it, or picked it up, and dropped it.'

'In that case, where is Brian? He didn't report in for work and he's not answering his mobile. I'm going back to the depot.'

'To do what?'

'I don't know. Talk to some of the other drivers. See if they know anything. Are you coming with me?'

'Do I have any choice?'

Marian jumped in the driving seat of the car and was already moving off by the time Georges was settled in his seat.

'For heaven's sake mind that bollard!' he shouted in alarm as Marian narrowly missed hitting an orange warning cone. 'I was right not to like your sister. She's nothing but trouble.'

'How can you be so heartless?'

'From years of looking out for myself,' Georges replied.

'If you feel like that, you can get out of the car, now.'

Marian slammed on the brakes so violently she dislodged her blonde hair from its usual elegant chignon.

'Darling.' Georges tucked a curl back behind her ear, 'I'm on your side. I want you to be happy; and if being happy means finding this wretched sister of yours then that is what I will do, so no more talk about throwing me out of the car in the middle of nowhere. Please? And would you mind driving a little more elegantly?'

'I'm sorry,' Marian apologised. 'I can't think straight.'

'In that case I will think for you,' Georges replied. 'I have had more practice at this sort of thing.'

Marian cast Georges a sideways glance. Although they were engaged, there were still large chunks of his past that were unknown to her. She suspected in his experience it wasn't unusual for people to disappear overnight.

'Now, the last known sighting of Sally was at the depot, wasn't it?'

'Since when, we've heard nothing from her.' Marian turned down Railway Approach and into the forecourt of the depot. Sara greeted them with a nervous smile from behind the reception desk.

'Has Brian Bartholomew turned up yet?' Marian demanded.

'No, but he'll be back. I'm sorry you can't find your sister, Miss Barr, but you told me yourself she doesn't know Brian.'

'I said she wasn't involved with him.'

The switchboard buzzed. 'I'm sorry; I'm busy. I can't help you any more.'

When Marian was about to protest further, Georges dragged her outside. 'Don't make a fuss,' he hissed. 'We don't want to get thrown off the premises.'

'I'm prepared to suffer that indignity

if it means finding my sister.'

'A wiser course of action would be if we were to take a leisurely stroll across the car park.'

'Why?'

The delivery park was a hive of activity. Vehicles trundled in and out constantly. Loud thuds accompanied the whine of equipment as hoists were raised and lowered to take delivery of yet another consignment of goods.

'There's a snack bar over there.' Georges pointed in the direction of a brightly lit mobile catering van.

'How can you think of food at a time like this?' Marian cast an agitated look around the yard.

'I'm not,' he replied, 'but there are a lot of drivers congregated around it, and where there are people there is gossip. Georges began to stride towards the plastic tables and chairs.

'Good day,' he greeted a group of men clustered round the burger bar. His casual charm won over their initial mistrust of a foreigner in their midst and they soon opened up with information after he bought a round of tea and sticky buns. No one, it seemed, particularly liked Brian Bartholomew. Several said it was nothing they could put their finger on, but something about him didn't quite add up.

'I think I caught a glimpse of your sister,' one of the drivers said to Marian. 'Drives a blue hatchback?'

'Yes,' Marian replied eagerly. 'That's her.'

'She was blocking the entrance.'

'I saw her hanging around too,' another put in. 'To be honest I thought she was one of Brian's lady friends. She shot off like a bullet when I hooted her.'

'When was this?'

'Can't remember exactly. It could have been sometime last week.'

'Have you seen her since?'

'No.' he shook his head.

'Do any of you know where Brian lives?' Georges asked.

'He doesn't socialise much,' another driver put in.

'He used to belong to a gun club.'

'And he used to boast that he was the greatest shot ever.' The man behind the burger bar grinned. 'He was modest like that.'

'He's got a gun?' Marian gulped at the thought of Brian possessing a firearm.

'He was always polishing the thing. Wouldn't let anyone else touch it. Ask Alf over there.' The burger man nodded towards a burly individual demolishing a bacon roll. 'He was a member of the club, still is I think.'

'That's right,' Alf agreed, replying to Georges' question. 'Brian was a member but he was suspended.'

'Why?' Marian clutched Georges' arm, making him wince.

'Something to do with conduct not in line with club rules and regulations. He wasn't too happy about it at the time. Said he'd done nothing wrong, but I seem to remember talk about him upsetting the farmer.'

'What farmer?' Georges asked.

'We used to shoot at a disused farmhouse. It was supposed to be clays, and only on official days with prior agreement with the farmer. There was a rumour that Brian set up a gallery in one of the barns and that he used to practise there with live ammunition whenever he fancied.'

'This farmhouse,' Georges said slowly, 'do you know where it is?'

'About twenty miles away. Why?'

'No reason.' Georges restrained Marian from butting in. 'Only, I know Mrs Rogers was looking to purchase a rural property in the area.'

'She wouldn't have been interested in this one. It was a run-down place. Hadn't been lived in for years. It had good outbuildings, but in the end health and safety condemned it and we had to stop using it for our target practice. Shame really. It was ideal. Not far off the main road.'

'What was it called?' Marian demanded.

Alf screwed up his face in thought. 'Something to do with a flower . . .

Buttercup? Can't remember. Sorry.'

'The burger man tells me you're enquiring about a blue hatchback?' a female traffic warden joined them at the table.

'That's right,' Marian greeted her eagerly.

'It may be nothing, but one's been parked illegally on double yellow lines outside the council offices. It was about to be clamped when I did my round.'

'Do you know the registration number?' Marian demanded.

'I have it somewhere.' The warden flicked through the pages of her notepad. 'Here it is.' She reeled off a number. 'Hope that helps. Hi, Alf. How's it going?' She sat down in the seat Georges had vacated.

'Come on.' Georges dragged Marian away from the catering van. 'We don't want to make a scene here.'

'You heard what she said.'

'Every word,' he said grimly.

'It's Sally's car. What do we do?'

'We mount a raid on this Buttercup

Farm, or whatever it's called,' Georges said calmly.

'How do we do that?' Marian asked. 'There are only two of us.'

'You forget.' There was a grim expression on Georges' face. 'I come from a regime of oppression and subterfuge. You learn to live by your wits when you dread the next knock on the door. Subterfuge is a skill that hasn't deserted me.'

In that moment Marian realised just how much she loved Georges. This was a side to him she had never seen before. He could be infuriating, vain, excitable and maddeningly charismatic, but he was the man by her side when she needed him. He believed in her and he wasn't going to desert her or question her sanity.

'Won't it be dangerous?' she asked in a half whisper.

'I told you I loved you,' Georges said softly. 'I'll do anything for you. The question is, are you up to the challenge?'

Marian raised her chin in defiance. 'Do you have to ask?'

Georges drew her body to his in a reassuring hug. 'Sally will be OK. You have my word.' His neck was soft against her nose. She inhaled the masculine smell of his flesh. His heartbeat raced against hers.

'But first,' his lips moved her hair, 'we have to get ourselves better equipped for guerrilla warfare.'

'Then you think she is at this Buttercup Farm?'

'It's as good a place to start as any. Now are you ready?'

In the distance a car backfired. It sounded like a gunshot.

20

'We'd better conceal the car under a tree,' Georges suggested as Marian bumped the vehicle down the rutted incline. 'Perhaps halfway along the track.'

It was starting to rain and the wind began to howl, a mournful wail reminiscent of a soul in torment. Marian shivered. Although they were in the heart of the country, there was no birdsong and no signs of spring. It was as if all wildlife had identified it as a place of evil and abandoned it long ago. Rarely had Marian seen a more desolate spot. The sky was grey with heavy clouds and in the distance she heard a rumble of thunder.

Georges indicated a passing place. 'Park here if you can.'

Marian swung the steering wheel to the left as the wipers swept across the windscreen.

'We're facing the wrong way for a quick getaway.'

'We can't risk turning round now in case we get stuck.' Georges shook his head. 'The ground's quite firm. Let's hope we don't have a problem.'

Marian's fingers shook as she turned off the engine. With the loss of warmth from the heater, cold began to seep into her legs. 'We don't even know if we're in the right place,' she said, shivering and massaging her cramped limbs.

'The sign at the top indicated it was Buttercup Farm, and it's our only lead.' A smile tugged the corner of Georges' mouth. 'This is quite like old times.'

'What is?' It was all Marian could do to get the words out, her teeth were chattering so hard.

Georges had insisted they wear black clothing: woolly hats pulled down low to conceal their hair, and smeared boot polish on their faces. His teeth flashed white against his darkened face. 'We were so hungry as kids we used to wait until nightfall, then take to the country-side and pinch whatever we could.'

'That's d . . . dishonest,' Marian stuttered.

Georges' eyes hardened to the colour of a winter sea. 'When you're starving you don't see it like that. The potatoes would only have been left to rot, the apples too. The farmers had enough to eat. We weren't robbing anyone who was hungry. We had to eat to survive. It was the only way.'

Marian put out a gloved hand and clasped his. 'I had no idea,' she whispered.

'There's a lot about me you don't know,' he added with a grim twist to of his mouth, 'and a lot you are about to find out. Before this little escapade is over I'll probably be demonstrating skills you never suspected I possessed, skills I had almost forgotten. Now, do we have everything?'

Before setting out, along with their dark clothing they had purchased a torch, a sturdy knife and a powerful pair of field binoculars.

'Keep down low,' Georges said, opening the passenger door and ducking his head. 'Follow me and don't use the flashlight unless you have to.'

Marian crouched behind him as he zigzagged from left to right down the muddy drive towards the derelict outbuildings. The recent snow made the going slippery, and more than once Marian bit down a cry as her feet slid away from her.

'Steady,' Georges admonished when she cannoned into his back for the second time.

'Can't get my feet to work properly.' She scrambled back onto her knees, wondering if she would ever get the smell of mud and boot polish off her skin.

Georges crammed bits of escaping blonde hair back under her woolly hat. 'All right now?' he checked.

Marian nodded.

'Right, on we go.'

They continued to make slow but

steady progress. Georges used the binoculars every few minutes to check for a reaction from the farmhouse. As they neared the buildings, he cursed.

'What is it?' Marian hissed behind him.

'Don't know. My foot's hit something.' He held up a tin can punctured by tiny dents. 'What do you make of this?'

'Are the holes what I think they are?' Marian's eyes widened.

Georges nodded grimly. 'Looks like someone's been indulging in target practice.'

'Do you think it's the gun club?' Marian asked.

'They don't come here anymore, and in any case they'd probably have proper targets. That delivery driver told us Brian used to hang around here on his own agenda and without the farmer's permission.'

'It's very quiet.' Marian sidled closer to Georges.

'Too quiet. I don't like the look of

things. Perhaps you should go back to the car,' he suggested, 'and wait for me there.'

'I'm not leaving you,' Marian protested.

'You'd be safer and it would put my mind at rest.'

'This thing was my idea and I intend being in for the kill.'

'You could have phrased that a bit better,' Georges replied, attempting a wry smile.

'Look,' Marian whispered, grasping his arm.

'What? Where?' He turned his head.

'There.' She pointed to a clump of trees behind the farmhouse.

'I don't see anything.'

A blast of wind caused the branches to sway, and they both caught a glimpse of white paintwork and the headlight of a delivery van.

'It's Brian's.'

'We can't be sure of that,' Georges cautioned her.

'It has to be. Who else would be

driving one of the delivery company's vehicles out here? This place can't be on anyone's regular route.'

'You're probably right.'

'And if he is here,' Marian's throat locked, 'he's got Sally with him. The police are going to have to listen to us now.'

'There isn't time to call them, and why should they listen to anything we have to say?' Georges demanded in an angry voice. 'They clearly thought we were a couple of cupcakes short of a picnic last time. We are going to have to do their dirty work for them and you are going to have to be very brave, my darling.'

'Are you saying you think Sally's dead?' Marian gasped.

'It's a possibility,' Georges admitted, 'but whatever the situation, we are in serious danger. Brian could be armed and I suspect he's close to losing it. He's a trained marksman on the run and he has the mindset of a killer. It doesn't get much worse than that.'

'I can't allow you to put your own life in danger for my sister.'

'We've come this far. We can't back out now.' Georges was grim-faced. He checked that the batteries in his torch were working properly and made sure the knife was still in his pocket. 'Ready?'

'Ready as I'll ever be. How about you?'

'I may be a bit rusty on technique but my adrenaline's pumping. We have reached the point of no return.'

From her kneeling position behind him, Marian launched her bulk against Georges. She wanted to absorb her body into his. She had so seriously misjudged him. He wasn't a vain aesthete, only used to making music. He was the bravest man she knew, and she could be sending him to his death.

He fell backwards from the impact of her body and landed in the mud. Marian rolled on top of him, her breath coming in harsh sobs. 'I love you so much it hurts.' She struggled to speak coherently. 'I never want to lose you. If we get out of this alive, let's go away without telling anyone and get married as soon as we can.'

'That's what I've been trying to persuade you to do all along.' Georges shifted position under her and kissed the shape of her ear through her woolly hat. 'Right now, however, we do have other priorities; and as I can't persuade you to desert me, can you bear to drag your body off mine and crawl the rest of the way forward on your stomach?'

Marian kissed his blackened nose. She was no longer cold. Her body was on fire with longing for him. 'What have you got in mind?'

'I don't know exactly, but we have to discover where Brian is hiding out and if Sally really is with him, so we need to search all the buildings.'

'We've lost our natural cover. It's all open space now.'

'If we can get as far as that bank,' he said, nodding towards a grassy mound, 'we're nearly there. We're going to have to be careful, but they won't be looking out for us. Now, radio silence. Just an expression,' Georges added when Sally looked puzzled. 'The slightest noise can shatter the peace and quiet, so watch where you're going and follow me.'

They crawled towards the bank. Marian was surprised no one could hear the rate of her heartbeat. To her it sounded like pounding drums.

'This is where it gets really nasty.' Georges directed his binoculars towards the outbuildings and peered through them.

'Can you see anything?'

'Not much. There's no sign of human life. We're going to have to make a dash for that cowshed. I'll go first. Watch what I do; then when I signal, you do the same.' He curled himself into a ball and scuttled across the scrubland, giving the appearance of a giant badger hurrying for cover. Inside the cowshed, Georges flashed his torch at Marian and beckoned to her. Taking a deep breath, she followed his example.

Georges put a finger to his lips as, biting down a cry of triumph, Marian reached her goal. He pointed to a discarded chocolate bar wrapper on the ground and raised his eyebrows. Marian nodded. There was other evidence of recent human occupation — a dried up tea bag, cake crumbs on the floor and a screwed up paper serviette decorated with silver hearts. Marian remembered seeing similar ones on Sara's desk back in the office. The dull ache of suspicion in her chest was growing stronger by the second. Sally was here. She could feel it in her bones.

Georges pointed with his finger, indicating that Marian should again follow him into the adjacent barn. If Marian had been left in any doubt before, what they discovered in the barn confirmed her worst fears. Piled in the corner was a pile of old rags and several spent cartridge cases, along with some mouldy hunks of bread and the body of a dead rat. She could see it had been shot, and it looked as though someone had tossed the carcass against the wall.

Georges clamped a hand over her mouth to stifle her cry of shock. She could feel his breath against her face. 'Don't lose control now.' He squeezed her arm. 'For Sally's sake.'

Marian nodded, struggling to control her breathing. Georges drew the knife he had purchased out of his jacket pocket and inched slowly forward. All the warmth left Marian's body. She didn't think she would ever feel warm again. In the distance the sound of vehicles roaring down the motorway sounded reassuringly everyday. It was hard to believe they were so near civilisation, yet here less than half a mile from a busy main road it was as if all social barriers had been deconstructed. They were in a world where nothing seemed real anymore.

She watched in horrified fascination as Georges paused by the open gap in the wall. It was as though he had been turned to stone.

'Stay exactly where you are,' a chilling voice ordered from the far side of the wall, 'otherwise I'll blow your brains out.'

21

'We meet at last, Mr Pascal. Over there,' a harsh voice barked, 'next to your sister-in-law. She doesn't look quite so beautiful now, does she? In fact neither do you. You make quite a pretty pair.'

'Sally?' Without a backward glance in Marian's direction, Georges lurched out of sight. 'It is Sally, isn't it?'

'Answer him, bitch,' Brian shouted.

Marian heard a moan and felt sick. A bubble of terror mingled with anger blocked her throat. She could only imagine what the brute had done to her sister. Every muscle in her body tightened as she waited for Brian to set his sight on her. She was prepared to fight him until the last breath left her body. The minutes ticked by. She heard Georges comforting Sally in a gentle voice, telling her that everything would be all right.

'Leave her alone,' Brian snapped, 'and no funny business. If you know what's good for you and her you'll do exactly as you're told.'

Scuffling noises followed. Marian's imagination went into overdrive as she tried to envisage what was happening. She clenched her fists and made a silent vow. If Brian was going to take them down, she was taking him with her.

'Now,' he breathed heavily, 'I'm going to make the knots really tight. Two for the price of one,' he sniggered. 'That should have your piano-playing girl-friend hot-footing back from Paris, or wherever she is.'

Marian gulped. She could hardly believe what she was hearing. Incredible though it was, it seemed Brian had thought Georges was up here on his own.

This was her only chance to get away and summon help before he realised his mistake, but there wasn't time to get to the car and drive back to the depot. She had to act now. Moving carefully, desperate not to make any noise, she began to sneak back outside, praying there were no more tin cans in her path to give her presence away.

Reaching her goal, she gulped a lungful of fresh air and doubled over. She hadn't dared breathe, but she had made it back outside. Now what? Looking round in wild confusion, she again caught sight of the delivery van parked behind the trees. Sweat was pouring off her and her breath was a mixture of heavy sobs and agonising stabs in the chest. If Brian suspected she was on the premises it would only take him a moment to find her. He knew the layout of his territory. She didn't. The van was her only chance.

Tensing her leg muscles, she tiptoed towards it. The driver's door was unlocked. She jumped in and ducked down on the front seat. Doubled up again, she struggled to breathe normally. She had to get her breath back before she could think straight. She had landed on a carton of half-eaten french fries. The greasy smell of stale fat made her want to vomit. She kicked out at a clutter of old pizza boxes and rotting hamburgers. Her foot slipped on cold coffee in the foot well as she tried to straighten up.

She groped around the dashboard but all she discovered was an open bag of peanuts and a chocolate bar. Any faint hopes she had entertained that the keys might be in the ignition were swiftly dashed. She could hotwire the engine, but opening the bonnet might attract Brian's attention and she couldn't risk it.

She crawled through to the rear of the van in search of a weapon. If she could find the wheel jack, maybe she could do something with that. Pushing aside a filthy old rug and a greasy pillow, she raised a fist in triumph as a flap in the flooring revealed a toolbox nestled in an alcove underneath. She opened it and lifted out a crowbar. It was so heavy she nearly dropped it. With animal-like grunts, she crawled back into the driver's cab and rested her head on the dashboard. Did she have the courage to take a swipe at Brian with the crowbar if she could catch him unawares? Hours of piano practice had toned her arm muscles and she was prepared to take the risk, but was she strong enough to take on a psychopath? The thought of Brian hurting Georges or Sally was enough to fuel her aggression, but they were both tied up and Sally was injured. Neither of them would be able to come to her aid.

Marian raised her head and stared at the array of switches ranged in front of her. The radio. Why hadn't she thought of it before? There had to be somebody on the other end. Frantically she flicked switches and pressed knobs, but with no success. All the lines were dead.

Her blood froze as she heard a gunshot from the farmhouse. There was no time to lose. She had to act now. Grabbing the door handle, she jumped out of the van. The only way out of this stinking mire was to do the job herself. Brian didn't know she was here. She had the advantage and a slim chance of overpowering him, and maybe she could get her hands on the gun. The odds weren't good, but she had Georges on her side.

Crawling round the back of the building, she heard Brian's taunting voice floating through a gap that had once been a window. 'No one comes up here much any more so we won't be disturbed.' He sounded chillingly normal. 'I used to shoot clays here. I was part of a syndicate. But they chucked me out. What do they know about anything? I was their best shot but my face didn't fit. Still, I showed them. I kept my twelve-bore shotgun and I'm a very accurate shot. See?'

There was the sound of another gunshot and a pinging noise. To Marian's untrained ear it sounded as though he was indulging in some target practice. In the distance she could hear the pressure of airbrakes being applied from lorries speeding down the motor-way. It was difficult to believe they were so close to the main road, but summoning help from that direction was not a viable option.

'You cannot keep us here forever.' It was Georges' voice. Marian bit down a sob of relief. He was alive. Brian hadn't harmed him.

'You can try and make a run for it if you like.' Brian sounded pleased at the prospect. 'But you're in the middle of nowhere and I've got the gun and, like I say, I'm a very accurate shot.'

His threats sent chills of fear down Marian's spine. This time she was unable to prevent a groan escaping her lips. She had to do something, and soon, before Brian totally flipped and they were all shot by a madman in a deserted farmhouse.

'What was that?' Brian snapped.

'I didn't hear anything,' Georges said.

'There's someone out there.'

'Then you'd better go and see who it is.'

'What are you up to?' Brian demanded.

'Nothing. My hands are tied.'

'You didn't come up here on your own, did you?'

'Why don't you go and find out?'

'You're trying to get rid of me.'

'Not at all,' Georges insisted, 'although I can think of better ways of spending my evening than sitting around discussing guns and unexpected guests with you.'

'Shut up,' Brian shouted.

'Anything you say.'

'You're confusing me. My head hurts. I did hear someone outside.'

'Then go and see who it is,' Georges again urged.

'I'm not leaving you two alone in here.'

'Then what are you going to do?'

Marian looked round. Georges was giving her a message. Somehow she had to lure Brian outside. It was the only way. Looking down at the ground, she found a large sharp stone, ideal for her purpose. Perched on the top of a tumbledown wall were some old tin cans that she suspected Brian had used for target practice. Without a second thought she hurled her missile and watched it soar through the air. Never had time passed so slowly. The stone seemed to hover in the air before it decided to lose height and bounce off the wall, taking two of the cans with it. They clattered to the ground.

'You're right,' Georges said as the noise subsided, 'We have a visitor. You'd better go and investigate.'

Roaring like an outraged bull, Brian thudded out of the farmhouse. Quick as a flash, Marian raced round the opposite side of the building and back through the barn.

Georges was lying trussed up on the floor of the cowshed, his hands and feet secured by twine. Curled up in a ball beside him was an unconscious Sally.

Dropping her crowbar Marian ran towards Georges.

'The knife,' Georges urged, 'get it out of my pocket before he comes back.'

Marian's fingers were so numb she couldn't work them. She fumbled with the zip of his jacket.

'Come on, we don't have all day.'

'I'm doing my best,' she sobbed.

She tugged at the knife finally freeing it up.

'What do I do now?'

'Cut.' Georges turned his back on her and held out his arms.

Marian began to saw away at his bonds securing his wrists

'Nothing's happening.'

'Keep going.'

'What's that animal done to Sally?'

'I've no idea but to my untrained eye she needs a doctor.'

Sally was curled up in a ball beside Georges. Like him her arms were tied behind her back. Her face was so dirty it was difficult to tell if Brian had harmed her.

'She is still breathing isn't she?' Marian's fingers began to cramp up as she tried to loosen Georges' bonds.

'She's alive that's all I can say. She

tried to speak to me but I think she passed out.'

'He didn't hit you did he?' Marian's emotions threatened to get the better of her.

'It would take more than a wacko with a gun to do me in.' Georges tugged at the rope.

'Very touching.' Brian was back, his bulk filling the doorway. 'So you're Marian Barr and you've come to rescue your sister and old Georges here. Well, you're wasting your time.'

Georges moved using his body to shield Marian.

'I'm afraid nothing's going to save your girl friend now Mr Pascal, despite the gallant gesture.'

'I wouldn't be too sure of that.'

'I would.'

Marian looked down to where she had dropped her crowbar. Brian hadn't noticed it. He hadn't noticed the knife either.

'Come away from him,' he ordered her.

'Do as he says,' Georges nudged Marian, his fingers tugging the knife blade from hers.

Warm blood seeped into the palm of her hand, as she made sure Georges had hold of the knife before leaving his side and inching towards the crowbar.

'Now you're being sensible.' Brian revealed his misshapen teeth in a parody of a smile.

'What have you done to my sister?' Marian demanded.

'She got nothing she didn't deserve.'

'Why are you doing this to us?'

'I shouldn't have thought you needed to ask.' A look of disgust crossed Brian's face. 'I had everything until your precious Peter arrived on the scene.' His eyes were glazed with anger. 'Then he took it all. I had to share even when I didn't want to. He was the favourite. Always winning gold stars for his music and his painting. Mum took on extra work to pay for his swimming lessons.' He was now working himself up into a rage. 'There wasn't enough money for lessons for me when I'd been at school but Peter wanted for nothing. He was her blue-eyed boy.'

'He was your brother.'

'He was your bastard.'

'I was married to his father,' Marian sobbed, but Brian was past listening.

'You didn't want him and neither did I. I got rid of him and now I'm going to get rid of you.'

'You're mad,' Marian hurled the words at him.

'Now that is a word I don't like to hear,' Brian replied in a terrifyingly calm voice. 'Everyone is mad, but there are degrees of madness. Who's to say I'm not as sane as you or your sister?'

'If you've harmed Sally, I'll kill you.'

Sally stirred at the mention of her name.

'It doesn't go like that, I'm afraid,' said Brian with an evil smile, 'I'm the man with the gun. Now, who's going to be first?'

He closed one eye and aimed at Marian.

'If you kill me how will you get any money?'

'Now that was a foolish remark.' Brian looked as though he were enjoying a secret joke. 'You're perfectly right of course. It would do no good killing you. You're my passport to freedom but you've just signed your sister's death warrant. She's no good to me.'

'Neither am I,' Georges said with a look of loathing on his face.

'I may let you live, I may not.' Brian reminded Marian of a cat playing with a mouse.

'Why do you have to kill anybody?' she asked in a hoarse voice.

'Your sister's been nothing but a nuisance from the start and,' he switched attention back to Georges, 'I don't like you.'

'The feeling is mutual.'

'Don't get lippy with me.'

'What have I got to lose?' Georges challenged.

'The police know we're here.'

Marian didn't know what game Georges

was playing but she knew it wouldn't do any good antagonising Brian.

'No they don't. There's no one outside. I checked.'

It had been a hopeless gamble and it hadn't paid off. Marian sagged against the wall.

'You're making my head ache.' Brian seemed to lose interest in pointing his gun at them. He flicked his dirty blond fringe out of his eyes.

'Why don't you sit down and rest? You've had a busy day.'

Marian went for the gentle touch in a last ditch effort to defuse the situation.

Neither of them saw Georges move. Finally freed of his bonds, he lunged at Brian. With a roar of mingled shock and pain Brian fell to the ground. Georges was the fitter and leaner but his feet were still tied together restricting his movement. The two men rolled over and over. Grabbing at her crowbar Marian raised it above her head.

It came down hard. She heard the crack of a bone. The gun went off.

22

Marian ran her fingers through Georges'
freshly shampooed wiry hair. His body
was still covered in bruises, like hers. A
frisson of pleasure worked its way up
Marian's spine as Georges snatched her
fingers away from his hair and proceeded
to kiss her naked flesh. The solid four-
poster rocked from the strength of his
embrace.

'You must promise never to involve
me in anything so adventurous again.'
Georges' kisses grew harsher and more
urgent.

'I had to rescue my sister.'

'I know but I've had enough of
murder and mayhem to last me a
lifetime.'

'Me too,' Marian agreed.

'It's been at least an hour since we
made love and I don't have to remind
you the artistic temperament needs

physical satisfaction on a regular basis,' Georges insisted.

'A rumour no doubt invented by a randy maestro,' Marian retaliated.

'Nonetheless you are aroused. I can feel it from the heat of your body against mine.'

Marian's head was spinning and her body ached and she could still smell boot polish in Georges' hair, yet never had she felt so glad to be alive. Dismissing all other thoughts from her mind she gave herself up to the pleasure of Georges' lovemaking.

★ ★ ★

Two weeks later they were married quietly in a secret ceremony with only a cleaning lady and her husband as witnesses.

After the events at Buttercup Farm hit the headlines the world's paparazzi went into overdrive and dogged their every move. The rescue of the famous Marian Barr's sister from the hands of a crazed killer by Marian and her fiancé, the equally celebrated Georges Pascal, had hit the headlines and caused a media sensation. The aftershocks rumbled on for weeks. Every day fresh revelations were dug up about Marian's past.

The story of her marriage to her first husband, the circumstances of his death and the adoption of Peter by Peggy Bartholomew and her husband had run and run. Grainy pictures of a young Marian, arm in arm with Valentin had also been dredged up from the archives.

There had been heartbreaking pictures of Peter published on line and reports of the fatal accident that had killed him re-hashed. Sally's criminal record had been reported in depth and even their father's accident discussed in detail. No part of Marian's past had been left untouched. Georges' past too had come under scrutiny.

His upbringing under a harsh regime of oppression and fear, his frequent clashes with the authorities, his defection to the west and his flamboyant lifestyle had been the subject of several in depth documentaries.

On their agents' advice, Georges and Marian had withdrawn from all professional engagements for personal reasons while the police went through the painstaking procedures of proving exactly what had happened at Buttercup Farm.

Everyone had been interviewed in depth and endless reports made out, signed, checked and re-checked until Georges had finally stormed out of his last interview, dragging Marian after him, citing an infringement of their human rights.

After that threat no one had dared take him on again.

The police enquiry revealed that Jack, Brian's stand in at the depot, had logged onto a radio wavelength in the control room and heard Marian desperately searching for a connection. He was trying to re-connect when the line went dead.

Seriously worried about Brian's whereabouts and the driver talk around the catering van regarding the whereabouts of Marian's sister he had alerted the police who had arrived at Buttercup Farm just as Brian's gun went off.

He had been killed instantly and the verdict had eventually been accidental death.

With reporting embargoes lifted the press had gone to town on Peggy Bartholomew, calling her the mother of a monster until she too had been forced into hiding.

After a week in hospital Sally had been discharged and in an attempt to patch up their marriage Ian had spirited her away to a secret holiday destination the whereabouts of which not even Marian knew.

And now it was the night of the charity concert. The date had been postponed several times but the organiser assured Marian and Georges it was a sell out.

'Even the weather is on our side,' she informed them when she came to check up on their star performers.

Although it was nearly ten o'clock in the evening it wasn't yet dark. The roses were in full bloom and their scent lingered on the night air. The concert-goers had brought sandwiches and eaten their picnics down by the lake. Marian and Georges had paid for a huge consignment of fresh strawberries to be delivered to Saltway Manor and a free punnet had been given to every ticket holder. It had been an evening of love and laughter and now everyone was preparing for the evening of music to begin.

The programme had been carefully selected after a brief video link discussion with the committee who were prepared to agree to anything Georges or Marian suggested.

'We thought now you're both super-stars,' the organiser Mrs Mitchell confessed self-consciously via the link, 'that you might not want to honour our previous arrangement. We would be disappointed but of course we would understand.'

'What do you mean?' Georges had asked in a chilling voice.

'At best the venue will be modest. There won't be any VIP reception or much in the way of facilities, just your fans and the changing rooms will be the mobile toilet block. It won't be what you're used to.'

'Mrs Mitchell,' Georges had flashed an angry look at the screen, 'if you still wish to remain on good terms with me and Miss Barr, you will never repeat a remark of that nature again.'

A flustered Mrs Mitchell had immediately backtracked.

'Of course. I understand. I only meant, it's, well, we're not very grand and,' she cleared her throat, 'the charity can only offer you modest expenses.'

'Which we refuse to accept,' Georges informed her, 'now can we get back to the matter in hand or would you prefer I turn off this wretched link thing?'

After that Mrs Mitchell had been putty in his hands.

'I feel sick with nerves,' Marian

admitted to Georges in their makeshift dressing room. Outside she could hear the orchestra warming up. 'In fact I have been sick.'

Georges kissed the white gold band on her wedding finger.

'Madame Pascal,' he tutted, 'you cannot throw a sickie now. This is going to be the night of your life.'

'That's what I'm afraid of. We've had so much adverse publicity.'

'I don't think this audience will throw our strawberries back at us and there's no such thing as adverse publicity. I should know.' Still sporting a purple bruise on his forehead, which gave him a slightly rakish air, Georges squeezed her hand. 'You don't need me to tell you there's only one way to dismiss the ghosts of our past and that's to face them front on do you?'

'No,' Marian admitted in a soft voice. 'It is time to move on.' She raised her eyes to his.

'I've never really thanked you have I?'

'What for?'

For all you did.'

'Your love is the only thanks I need,' he replied. 'Now are you ready? Your public is waiting.'

From the moment the two of them stepped onto the stage hand in hand, the response was overwhelming. Marian and Georges received a standing ovation before either of them performed a note.

Richard had leaked the news of their marriage a few hours before the performance and bouquets of flowers and red roses were being tossed onto the makeshift stage. The rafters rang with cheers as an army of volunteers scooped up the flowers while the orchestra acknowledged the applause by adding their own accolade, the violin section tapping their bows against their music stands.

As the applause died down and Marian settled in front of the piano she felt such joy, as she had never known before. Soon the reasons for the radiant bloom on her cheeks and the extra sheen to her hair would be apparent as would her gain in weight and bouts of sickness, but for the moment only two people knew about the new life growing inside her.

Her gown had been cleverly fashioned to disguise her condition but no doubt Richard would arrange another of his convenient leaks to the world's media when he deemed the time was right.

Marian arranged her music. From the podium Georges glanced across at her, winked then teased the orchestra by camping up a few imaginary warm up gestures. A ripple of laughter ran through the audience. As usual he held them in the palm of his hand.

Marian smiled at his antics then bit her lip as she received a violent and unexpected kick in the pit of her stomach. It was so strong she was forced to stop and catch her breath. Georges glanced at her with an anxious frown.

Patting her stomach in an intimate

gesture which he immediately understood he waited a few moments then
checking she was ready he raised his
arms.

Marian flexed her fingers. It would
seem her husband and her unborn child
were both anxious to start. She nodded
towards Georges.

Soon they would have to share their
news with the world but for the
moment it was their secret.

THE END

We do hope that you have enjoyed reading this large print book.

Did you know that all of our titles are available for purchase?

We publish a wide range of high quality large print books including:
Romances, Mysteries, Classics
General Fiction
Non Fiction and Westerns

Special interest titles available in large print are:
The Little Oxford Dictionary
Music Book, Song Book
Hymn Book, Service Book

Also available from us courtesy of Oxford University Press:
Young Readers' Dictionary
(large print edition)
Young Readers' Thesaurus
(large print edition)

For further information or a free brochure, please contact us at:
Ulverscroft Large Print Books Ltd.,
The Green, Bradgate Road, Anstey,
Leicester, LE7 7FU, England.
Tel: (00 44) 0116 236 4325
Fax: (00 44) 0116 234 0205

VET IN DEMAND

Carol Wood

For Elissa Hart, the shock of her father's sudden death is bad enough. To find his veterinary practice in such a poor state, both financially and with dated equipment, is just as upsetting. The only way to save the practice is to take on a partner able to make a real investment — and Adam Kennedy is willing to do just that. Can Elissa reconcile her resentment of Adam and his bold ideas with her growing attraction to him?

THE SHAPE OF SUMMER

Barbara Cust

When Anna Blakeney is offered the temporary job of looking after the Chatham children, Sara and Jeremy, her guilty feelings about the deaths of their parents in the car which Anna's father was driving make it impossible for her to refuse. She instantly dislikes the children's half-brother and guardian, Drewe, but while he is away she reckons she can sort out her problems with her boyfriend Ricky. Then Ricky meets someone new, and Anna is surprised to find that her own passions have changed in the most unpredictable way . . .

ESCAPE FROM THE PAST

Iris Weigh

Driving northward in the hope of leaving behind her old life and painful memories, Clare Bowers takes a wrong turn in the mist and ends up in a ditch, from which she is rescued and taken to stay at Moorlands Farm. The owners have had their own tragedies in the past, and there is still a bitter feud between them and the Laytons at the nearby farm. Then Clare meets the darkly handsome Richard Layton, and her past threatens to overtake her again . . .

TAKE A CHANCE

Sheila Holroyd

When Tessa unexpectedly loses her job, she tries to console herself by impulsively going on holiday to Spain, hoping that a sun-soaked restful break will help her face the future. But instead she finds herself involved in the affairs of Tom, an Englishman who has settled in the country, and two children who have apparently been abandoned by their father. She does her best to help them all, but will Tom's past stop her from finding happiness?

THE HOLLY BOUGH

Pamela Kavanagh

When Catrin and her family are taken on as farm help, word soon spreads that she has 'a winning way with livestock, and a rare touch with plant and herb cures'. But Catrin's burning desire is to find the person who abandoned her as a baby on a pile of straw in a stable one Christmas. It is an obsession that even puts at risk the future she might have with the local smith, Luke . . .